VISIONS OF DESTINY
Copyright ©2022 Susan Harris
All rights reserved.

ISBN: 978-1-63422-517-5 (paperback)
ISBN: 9781634224994 (e-book)
Cover Design by: Gem Promotions
Typography by: Gem Promotions
Editing by: Chris Kridler
Proofing by: Ashley Brilinski

VISIONS OF DESTINY

SICARIUS SECURITY BOOK 3

SUSAN HARRIS

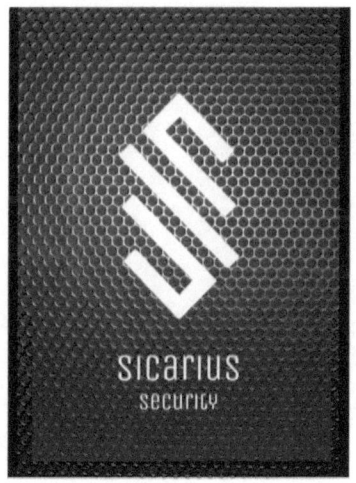

Flectere si nequeo superos, Acheronta movebo
"If I cannot sway the Heavens, I will raise Hell"
Jasmine Cavanagh

Lupus non timet canem latrantem
"The wolf is not afraid of a barking dog."
Roman Lowe

CHAPTER ONE

Jasmine

"Is it still classed as murder if I give them a heads-up?"

Jasmine Cavanagh glanced around the clearing she had been stuck in for the last seven months and growled to herself. The words she spoke didn't so much as echo in the silence that surrounded her. Jasmine was pissed as all hell that someone had managed to pull a sleeping beauty spell out on her, considering she saw the future.

But you've stopped seeing your own future, haven't you? How could you see this coming?

The thoughts did little to console Jasmine about her failure to see this coming, and she was hard on herself for it. Perhaps that was why she had just sat down in the clearing for a few weeks and not even bothered to try and find a way out?

Whoever had whammied her with the spell knew Jasmine and her family well enough to propel her to a place very few people knew about. The place where Malakai, her eldest brother, had come up with the idea that they should use the skills they had to be assassins in the Inferna community, the supernatural beings that lived in the shadows of the humans around them.

They had sat around the same fire where Jasmine now sat, but this time, Jazz was all alone. Night was never-ending, and time passed so slowly around her that Jasmine hoped it was only the seven months she estimated and not years she had been trapped here.

She missed her brothers: Kai, with his calculated brilliance and kindness; Dylan, with his reckless nature and heart of solid gold; and Zeke, their blooded brother who considered himself a monster, yet, like Dylan, had a massive heart underneath the gruff exterior. She missed the newest additions to their lives, Keeva and Scarlett.

Hell … she even missed trading barbs with the wolf.

Maybe she really was losing her damn mind.

Jasmine had missed all her favourite holidays. Her and Dylan's Halloween, Christmas, and New Year parties were legendary, and Jasmine spent months planning them. Jasmine loved the human holiday of Christmas the best, and she prided herself on giving the best gifts. Her brothers, who only celebrated because Jazz loved it so much, made sure to humour her.

Tossing a twig into the fire, Jasmine blew out a breath as she glanced around the clearing. After her initial shock, Jasmine had tried to find a way out, but this bullshit world was a loop that always brought her right back to the very spot she sat in now. No matter how far she walked or in what direction, she ended up back here. Looking on the bright side, at least there was no hunger, no bloodlust, and no tiredness.

Weirdly, she was aware of everything going on in her room, even if she was unable to make her body react. Like right now, she knew the guard dog was sitting on the chair by the window, flicking the pages of a book and drinking something. Roman never spoke to her, apart from one time when he got angry and told her to stop taking this lying down and fight back. This small connection had helped keep her from going completely insane. It also helped her track the days, assuming of course that her connection wasn't a weird glitch and in fact there were days where she was completely unaware of anything. Magic could be weird like that, but she had decided to focus on the positive.

Everyone came to spend time with her. Scarlett and Zeke

came to update her on baby Grayce. Malakai spoke to her in their native Norwegian, telling her about the day-to-day business. Dylan made sure to tell her, with blinkered focus, about Dante's, her beloved nightclub where she indulged in her passion for music. Keeva had stepped up to try and help Dylan manage the assassin side of Sicarius Security, yet as much as she loved hearing it all from them, it made her miss being awake more and more.

Jasmine felt her brother's presence as he came in the door, coming to press a kiss to her forehead, before she felt the dip in the mattress as Kai perched himself next to her. Jasmine could almost picture him now, stretching his legs out in front of him, then folding his arms behind his head as if he were using them as a pillow.

"You can talk to her, Roman. She can hear everything you say to her. She's probably listening right now."

There was a stretched silence as Jasmine heard Roman close his book before he answered Malakai. "Like I told Dylan, it's no fun when she can't answer me back. If she wants to have a conversation with me, Jasmine needs to cop herself on and wake herself up."

Jasmine growled to herself at his haughty tone, knowing Roman couldn't hear her as she gritted her teeth, prickling as Malakai chuckled softly while Roman told Malakai that he was gonna go for a run but would be back first thing to cover so the vampires could sleep.

It had utterly fascinated her that Roman still felt the call of the wolf, especially since the former military Inferna couldn't shift. When Dylan had asked him about it, Roman explained that the wolf was still inside of him, felt the urge to run and hunt as if it could break free of the confines of the human form, even if it never would.

It infuriated Jasmine that the more she learned about Roman Lowe, the more she was reminded of the blistering kiss they had shared when Jasmine had used the excuse of

Scarlett's drunken slip of power to indulge in her visceral need to know what those soft lips of his felt like against her own.

He wasn't ruffled by her smart mouth and wit, just fired back with his own, an easy smile on his handsome face. Her hands itched to tumble her fingers through his dark shoulder-length hair and to feel the roughness of his stubble on her skin. The taste of his blood had addicted her, like the finest of wines, and as much as Jasmine tried to deny it, she wanted her fangs in the thick of his neck again, to be swallowing his blood, his hands on her.

And it pissed her off that she wanted him so badly.

The prophetess will lose herself to a wolf like no other.

It will either be her end or her awakening.

The words were spoken to Jasmine over thirty years ago, when she had gone to kill a warlock who was using the bones of children in his spells. She had found herself crossing paths with a witch who, like her, could see the future. Jasmine had felt compelled to talk to her as her own visions had become scattered and unfocused, and she had this sense of dread in her chest.

"You are so focused on trying to see the future that you are strangling your gift. You cannot force destiny to be revealed to you, little seer. Forcing it will only cause you to anger those who give you the gifts and then, you may lose them altogether."

"Please," she had begged the witch. *"Just give me a glimpse, and I will stop trying to force it."*

The witch had grinned, revealing a mouth of blackened teeth as she replied. "The prophetess will lose herself to a wolf like no other. It will either be her end or her awakening."

Then Jasmine was shown a vision of herself running through the forest, running away as something snarled and growled behind her, and as she came to the edge of a cliff, Jasmine had turned to see a flash of amber eyes before she tumbled over the edge of the cliff.

Thirty years of avoiding werewolves, and one walked into

Sicarius Security to apply for a job just when someone with a vendetta against her family had started to make themselves known. This had made her totally suspicious of Roman, but the stupid wolf had proven himself time and time again.

Jasmine might give the impression she was an airhead DJ who was happy to let her brothers do all the heavy lifting, but she made it her purpose that everyone not know that she was more than just the sister of Malakai and Dylan.

It was why no one apart from those closest to her knew that the assassin code-named The Widow was in fact Jasmine. She liked it that way, but she suspected Roman was starting to see past her act, and it unnerved her.

The prophetess will lose herself to a wolf like no other.

It will either be her end or her awakening.

Jasmine shook herself and got to her feet. She might want to have fun naked sexy time with Roman, but there was no way in hell she was going to tempt fate and risk impending doom just because she wanted to get laid.

Nope …

Jasmine brushed the grass off her butt as she walked around the fire and warmed her hands on the flames, listening as Roman strode out the door, his footsteps heavy, yet Jasmine knew that if he wanted to skulk about unnoticed, the wolf knew how to do that.

When Jasmine heard the door shut, Kai sighed, his fingertips grazing her cheek. "I think that werewolf sleeps less than we do. I have no doubt that after his run, he will be straight on the phone to Dylan or Isolde to find out if he is needed elsewhere."

Jasmine cocked her head to the side as Malakai continued. "Come on, Jazz. We need you. Come back to us. We know you can hear us. We know that you are listening. I find myself adrift not knowing how to play the big brother and ride in to rescue you, knowing that you can protect yourself. You are the glue that keeps us all together, Jazz."

"It must perplex him so, not being the one to solve the problem."

Jasmine spun around, her hair whipping against her face as she moved, bracing herself for an attack, but all she could see was a shadowy outline of a hooded figure. Sniffing the air, Jasmine wasn't able to catch any scent other than the fire. She glared at the figure, who must have been the one to cast this enchantment on her. His tone was robotic, like he was trying to disguise his voice from her.

"Dude, seriously? This is getting old now. Are you so threatened by my awesomeness that you had to use an outdated whack spell to keep me out of the fight?"

"I have no fear of you, seer, other than your gift to try and see what my next move will be. The only question I have is whether or not you are smart enough to work your way out of here before I cut the child from the succubus's womb?"

"You won't get near Scarlett or the baby."

Even though Jasmine couldn't see his face, she could just feel his smile. "Oh, but I already have. Have the family not told you that I was standing right in front of Ms. Russell and I could have gutted her there and then outside the coffee shop? The banshee could not have stopped me. The obscurum could not stop me before I cut his child from the succubus."

Obscurum.

Darkness ... but why would this thing be calling Zeke darkness?

Jasmine laughed. "Your mistake was testing to see if you could get close unnoticed without acting on it. Scarlett will be locked up tight inside Sicarius Security until that kid is born, and you won't be able to get within the walls."

"The banshee managed. Even if she did not manage to kill your Malakai." The shadowy figure swayed, and Jasmine prepared herself once more to attack. "Without you, they will not see me coming. The empath is next for the slaughter."

Jasmine lunged forward as the figure dissipated into the

nothing, leaving Jasmine alone again in the vast emptiness as she snarled in utter frustration, especially since she could hear the son of a bitch laughing at her. Then words from the real world suddenly demanded her attention.

"What was it you told me once, Jazz, when I was struggling under the pressure of keeping Zeke from diving further into oblivion? The only way forward is through."

Jasmine rolled her eyes at Malakai and his Yoda words of wisdom, even if her brother couldn't see her. Letting loose a scream, Jasmine sank back down to the ground and rested her chin in her hands. It seemed useless. There was no way out of the hellhole, and her family was in danger.

The shadow had said that Dylan was next. Her brother was wicked smart, but his ability to feel others' emotions and take those emotions into himself meant he would sometimes be a little reckless. Jasmine had held her brother in her arms when he sank into someone else's depression. She had tried to make him laugh when he was consumed by anger.

Jasmine wanted to protect Dylan like he and Malakai had done with her, and to do that, she had to get out of this fucking hellhole.

Jasmine got back to her feet and kicked at the dirt as she sensed Keeva come into the room, and while she did not have the gifts that Dylan had, Jasmine could almost feel the happiness radiating from her brother.

"Still nothing?"

"Still nothing," Malakai responded, the sheer volume of sadness making Jasmine's chest ache.

Jasmine heard the soft press of lips, ashamed at the flash of jealousy that rippled through her. She kept it hidden most of the time, but Jasmine longed to have what Malakai and Keeva had, what Scarlett and Zeke had. She wanted someone who knew her and loved her all the same. The pang of guilt at feeling jealous made her dip her head, but she had been alone for such a long time, and even when she was with someone, they only knew a little portion of who she was.

Her ex, a vampire who wanted to be more successful in his vampire life than he had achieved in his mortal one, had tried to mould her into this trophy girlfriend. Jasmine had suspected that he had only tried to seduce her because he wanted to get closer to Malakai.

Duke had started small, chastising her for the unladylike way she spoke, commenting on her clothes and makeup, being jealous of her relationship with Zeke, even though Jasmine explained numerous times it was strictly platonic. He despised it when other men looked at her, but Jasmine found she didn't care if other women looked at him.

When Malakai had sent him back to the UK, his home country, he'd suggested that Jasmine should go with him because her life was not exactly riveting without him. Jasmine had ended the relationship there and then, but that hadn't stopped him from pursuing her still.

Then Jasmine had gone hunting for a warlock and found her destiny was tied to a wolf.

She'd kept her distance from all men since then.

And women, too, for that matter.

"You haven't eaten much this week in the way of real food. Come and sit down with the family. They could use your calming presence right now."

Malakai chuckled, a warm and comforting sound. "Calming presence? I do not recall you calling me calming last night when you threw a phone at my head."

"I said *they* need your calming presence. And I threw the phone at your head to get your attention because we've also barely seen each other all week."

Jasmine felt the bed shift as Malakai rose. "I'm sorry. I have been trying to spread myself too thin. With Scarlett now on bedrest, Zeke is a little volatile."

"It's okay, Cavanagh. I know what I signed up for. But let's go eat. And then maybe, a few hours' sleep."

"Going to bed sounds like a marvellous idea."

It was Keeva's turn to laugh then, making that little pang in her chest hurt again.

"Then let's go eat first. Build up your stamina."

"I don't like leaving her by herself," Malakai admitted as Jasmine heard his footsteps move away from the bed.

"I know. But you will be no good to her if you pass out due to lack of food and blood."

The couple left the bedroom, leaving Jasmine alone. Her head began to throb as if a vision was trying to make its way through whatever mojo the spell was working and failing, leaving Jasmine with that lingering hangover feeling. She tried to reach out for it. A pain stabbed behind her eyes as she hissed into the night.

Oh, Jasmine was pissed. She was done playing around. She needed off this ride right now.

Studying her surroundings, Jasmine thought back to what Malakai had said. *The only way forward is through.*

There was nothing for her to go through to get out of this hell-forsaken place. The crackling of the fire snared her attention, and Jasmine almost smacked herself for her stupidity. Every spell had a way out if you were smart enough to see it, and what better way to have the only means of escape be in the one thing most vampires were terrified of, apart from a solid gold stake.

Fire.

Jasmine glanced at the flames, striding forward to thrust her hand into them, and yelped as her fingers burnt. Pain blistered her hand, yet Jasmine, despite the prick of fear, held her nerve. She readied herself for the onslaught of pain, then rolled her shoulders back as she prepared to walk into the fire.

"I really liked this T-shirt," Jasmine mumbled, then stepped right inside the flames.

The red-hot flames seared her skin, and she couldn't hold back a scream of agony as the scent of her burnt flesh permeated the air. Jasmine considered stepping back, getting out. However, deep down she knew this was what she needed to do in order to get home and protect her family.

As suddenly as the pain started, it was over, and Jasmine sat upright in her bed, her vision blurring as her gift flooded her with flashes of images. She saw the shadowy figure clutching a small item in his arms and a dagger poised over her tiny body.

The shadow lifted his head and stared directly at Jasmine, his smile familiar before he vanished, leaving her to stare into eyes of amber and the snarling maw of a wolf.

Then the vision faded, and Jasmine blinked her eyes to focus on her room.

Hours had seemingly passed since Malakai had been here, for she sensed the daylight outside her blackout curtains. It seemed her thoughts on how time passed there may have been right, but there was nothing she could do even if that was the case. For now, she would let her family rest before she rallied the troops.

Jasmine was back and ready to kick some serious ass.

CHAPTER TWO

Roman

ROMAN'S RUN HAD NOT SATED THE BEAST CLAWING AT HIM FROM the inside.

Gritting his teeth as he punched the bag hanging from the family's personal gym, he tried to get some of the coiled aggression out of him before he had to start dealing with people. His bosses, vampires, were locked up for the daylight hours, and Roman would ensure that any matters that needed handling during that time were sorted.

Before Malakai Cavanagh retired for the day, he had made Roman get some sleep in the tiny guest bedroom that used to be Scarlett's before she moved to her own floor with Zeke. He had his own apartment, but it made sense to stay at the Sicarius headquarters while there was a threat looming.

They were no closer to finding out who was after the vampires and why they wanted Scarlett and Zeke's kid. And the one vampire who might be able to shed some light on things was acting like Sleeping Beauty.

Roman felt the growl rumble in his chest as he punched the bag, hard. The chains that held it suspended groaned but didn't break. Steadying it with his hands, Roman closed his eyes and inhaled a breath, his mind drifting to the smart-mouthed vampire who had burrowed under his skin and taken root.

From the very first moment he had met Jasmine Cavanagh and been on the receiving end of her sharp tongue, he could not get her out of his mind. Within minutes of them meeting, she had called him a dog, her dislike for his kind blatantly obvious, but he had happily traded banter with her, and his easy reactions seemed to confound her, so Roman kept it up.

He had the distinct impression that she was used to men, her brothers included, fawning at her feet, and no man would ever be much in her eyes if they didn't push back at least a little when she pulled.

And then there was that kiss.

His entire body had come alive when Jasmine had dragged his head down and kissed him hard on the lips, a bare lick of her tongue along the seams before she jerked back. She dismissed it as a result of a drunk Scarlett's succubus powers slipping, but Roman had seen her intent in Jasmine's eyes.

An image of Jasmine, her fangs in his neck, her body rocking against his, punched through him, causing Roman to suck in a shaky breath. He had wanted to strip her naked there and then, letting her slide down his rock-hard cock, her tight, wet core fisting him so good.

Shaking away the images of a naked Jasmine, he yanked his tee over his head and wiped the sweat from his brow. Malakai had told him to make himself at home, so he decided to head to the kitchen and feed the only appetite he could right now, just as his phone rang.

Walking over to the bench where he had stashed his personal items, he glared at the private number message that flashed on the screen, then pressed the answer button. "Lowe."

"Hey baby, you miss me?"

Roman rolled his eyes at the playful, teasing tone as he retorted, "Does your wife know you are calling up other men and calling them baby?"

"Who the hell do you think told me to call you? I believe

Abbie's exact words were, 'You haven't heard from your work wife in a few weeks. Call Roman.'"

Roman laughed as he heard the affection in Conor's tone, knew that there was no way his buddy would dare even contemplate straying from his missus, and that was without even considering Abbie was extremely talented with a blade. Besides, Conor and Abbie had been married for almost fifty years now, and they still acted like the first day Roman had introduced them. Conor had fallen for his wife there and then.

They had danced around one another for months after, until Conor got himself shot on a mission and Abbie helped nurse him back to health. Conor and Abbie were part of Roman's elite squad, one so classified that only the top tier of government knew they existed. Roman and Conor had been friends for years before ending up in the same unit, a covert team of supernaturals who went on missions no human could survive.

"Hiro's birthday is next weekend. We were hoping you would show. We haven't seen ya in ages, bud."

Roman scrubbed a hand down his face. "I'll be there. It's part of the deal. We don't miss important dates."

When Roman had recruited them all to the team, he had made certain stipulations. They never went a month without checking in, and they celebrated major events together. If they needed headspace, they came to him, because this was a family rather than a team. That was how Roman had operated, and it had kept them alive. And while they might not be active anymore, or more likely, the government had no use for them just yet, Roman made sure to check on them every so often.

"I know you have shit going on there, but the full moon isn't far away. Come run with us. It's always fun to watch Ezra rage because you beat him on two legs when he's on four. The girls like to make bets on when his head might explode."

Roman grunted out a bark of laughter even as that punch to his gut threatened to undo him. Conor and Ezra, both werewolves who didn't even consider Roman less because he couldn't shift, made the moons less lonely. He ran with them as if he had paws and fur, even when it was just flesh and bones he had.

He couldn't stop the memories of his pack's reaction to his latency, from the beatings from the older wolves to the multiple tests and medical appointments to make sure that the defect that Roman brought to the pack was not replicated. His own mother was banned from carrying another pup, especially when his father had managed to have another pup with his mistress.

The fact that he was the alpha's son made matters even worse. He felt the call of the moon, the urge to change, the pain when the wolf inside him raked its claws, trying to get free.

When Roman turned thirteen, he had experienced a growth spurt and was now taller and broader than his peers. He made sure he was as deadly on two feet as he could have been on four, winning dominance challenge after challenge. And when it became clear that in a few short years, Roman would be strong enough to challenge his father's position as Alpha, his father had kicked him out of the pack, claiming that he could not keep him there, on the chance that whatever curse bound him to two feet would be passed down to any young he might have.

Three weeks later, Roman had signed up for the army, and the rest was history. He considered himself a lone wolf, but if a wolf needed a pack to survive, Conor and the rest of his team were his pack, no doubt about it, even if only half of them were wolves.

"Sure, we can sort something out when we meet up for Hiro's birthday. The usual place?"

Roman could hear the smile in Conor's tone as he said, "Sure, where else would we go? See ya next week, wifey."

Roman was still laughing after Conor disconnected, shaking his head as he strapped on his watch and headed for the door of the gym. He pulled open the door and sucked in a breath as a deliciously intoxicating scent hit him like a two-by-four.

Wildflowers and sunshine, that was what the blond vampire smelled like, as she stood by the fridge and chugged from a bottle of blood. She wore the same pyjama shorts and a matching tee in a bright pink, and he watched as blood dripped down her front. She growled when the bottle was drained, and Roman realized it was in frustration when he spied the row of empty bottles on the counter.

"Jasmine."

The moment her name fell from his lips, she jerked her head in his direction, and her gaze was pure molten red, filled with hunger. She wiped her mouth with the back of her hand, her eyes never leaving his. It gave him a thrill to see the way her eyes then roamed over his naked skin, slick with sweat, before she snapped her gaze back to his face.

"Hungry."

Jesus, that tone shot straight to his cock as Jasmine shook her head and reached for another bottle of blood.

"I think if you've drank all that, darling, and are still hungry, then you need something from the source."

He strode toward her, tossing his tee on the couch, noting how the vampire retreated, almost suppressing a grin as she stared at the pulse in his neck. He wanted to feed her. He wanted to be the only one who fed her. The thoughts of her drinking from another male made all his possessive traits push forward.

"I'm not drinking from you, mutt."

Roman chuckled at the remark, delight in his chest at the fact she was still her, still the same gorgeous, intelligent woman with a wit that was biting even without trying. This was what he had been waiting months for, to hear that sarcasm in her tone, see that jaunty expression on her face. This was why he had told Malakai it was no fun talking to her if she couldn't answer back.

"Beggars can't be choosers, vampire. You need a hot vein, and here I am."

"I'll get a human," she grunted out as Roman grinned.

"Now that would involve waking your brothers. And while they ask you a million questions, you'll still be hungry. A little bite won't kill you, love."

Roman stalked toward her, his body thrumming with the anticipation of it, causing his heartbeat to quicken, and damn if Jasmine's eyes didn't darken at the sound of it. She looked like she was trying very hard to find a reason to not drink from him, but after seven months of watching her sleep, Roman needed this as much as she did.

Closing the distance between them, Roman reached for her, his palms finding her hips, and hoisted her up on the counter so that they were on eye level. He trailed his hands down to rest them on her thighs, feeling smug satisfaction as Jasmine shivered. Roman felt his skin get tight as he pushed apart her legs to step in closer. Jasmine's hands gripped the counter hard enough for the stone to crack.

"What are you doing?" Jasmine asked, a quiver in her tone.

"I'm getting in real close, Jasmine. The way you've been eyeing my neck, I wanted you to have easy access."

Roman tilted his head, his shoulder-length hair sliding off the nape of his neck, and Jasmine sucked in a breath. When she tried to keep a distance between them, Roman yanked her forward. Her legs instinctively went around his waist as he ducked his head, and Jasmine had to place her palms on his chest to steady herself.

Their gazes clashed and sucked all the oxygen from the room, leaving Roman gulping in a breath, his pulse quickening as Jasmine leaned in and her nose grazed the curve of his neck. This time, it was Roman that shivered. She wiggled closer, the heels of her feet digging into the backs of his thighs as she trailed her hands up his chest, into his hair and then tugged him down more.

But she still didn't bite him.

It was torture all in itself, the waiting, the needing for her to sink those fangs into his neck and feel the pull as Jasmine swallowed. The first time she drank from him, he had been addicted to it there and then, but it was the vampire he was addicted to.

Her teeth grazed his skin as Roman snaked a hand into her blond locks and held her to him. "That's it, Jazz. That's exactly what you want."

Her snarky response was muffled against his skin, but then Jasmine licked over his pulse, and any retort he might have shot off disappeared from his mind.

And again, she still didn't bite him.

He rotated his hips, showing Jasmine just how much this foreplay was affecting him, and that was what undid his vampire. With an animalistic snarl, Jasmine bit into the flesh at his neck, hard, painful even, causing Roman to hiss, but Jasmine was clawing at him to get him closer, as if she couldn't get enough of him.

As she drank, Roman slipped an arm around her waist to hold them as close as they could get with the barrier of clothes. His other hand held Jasmine's head to the curve of his neck, even as he angled his body to give her better access. Jasmine tightened her legs around his waist, and Roman thought he was going to explode there and then.

Roman was seriously considering stripping Jasmine of

those pink shorts and finding out if she tasted as good as she smelled right now. His heart beat in time with the hard swallows until he started to feel the effects of it, his brain fogging and his strength wavering.

The wolf in him howled, lying down to tilt its head in a drowsy state.

"Jasmine, that's enough for now."

The vampire snarled. "More."

Roman tangled his fingers in her hair and yanked her head back, dragging her teeth from his flesh, and it burned. She snapped her teeth in response, blood still dripping from the puncture wounds at his neck. Jasmine tried to get closer, but Roman needed to distract her from the blood, so he pressed his lips hard to hers, just lips against lips, tasting his own blood before he pulled back to see some blue begin to creep back into her eyes.

Those eyes of hers closed for a second, as if she needed a minute, then Jasmine leaned in and licked the curve of his neck, and they both groaned. Leaning back as Roman slid his palms up her bare thighs, Jasmine opened her eyes.

She glanced down and then back up at him, her cheeks flushed from the blood she had just drunk. "Looks like you enjoyed that way more than I did. Ugh, now I won't get the taste of chihuahua out of my mouth for days."

Roman smirked as he leaned in, still dizzy but relishing the opportunity to finally have this back-and-forth with her. "Keep telling yourself that, Jazz. Deny it all you want. But if I was to dip a finger inside you right now, I know that you are as wet as I am hard. I can smell you, and now I want a bite."

Jasmine gasped as she untangled herself from around Roman's torso and pushed him away, as if she needed to put some distance between them, but she couldn't douse the heat in her gaze. She pushed off the counter as Roman reached out to steady himself, dots dancing in his eyes.

Shit, Jasmine had taken more than he expected, but he hadn't wanted her to stop.

"Well, it's been seven months of not drinking or any physical contact. I'd get wet hearing my vibrator start up. Don't let it go to your head, wolf."

Roman grinned as Jasmine glanced at the elevator, and seconds later it opened, Malakai stepping into the room, dressed in sweatpants and a tee, then glancing from Jasmine to Roman.

"Am I interrupting something?" the vampire asked with a smirk of his own.

"Yes, thank you. God, Kai, it's good to see you!"

Roman watched as the siblings embraced, his legs feeling like lead as he tried to move but found that his energy was sapped.

Turned out he didn't need to run until his legs gave out because all he needed was a drop-dead gorgeous vampire sucking on his neck. He needed to sit down or he was going to keel over.

Gripping the countertop, Roman watched as Malakai checked Jasmine over, asking her if she was okay, and Jasmine replied that she was. Malakai asked her to tell him what had happened, and Jasmine flipped her hair off her shoulder, telling her brother that she would wait for everyone to wake up because she didn't want to have to repeat herself.

Malakai glanced at Roman, then back at Jasmine. "How much did you take?"

"Not a lot." Jasmine snorted before she admitted sheepishly without looking in his direction, "Maybe more than I should have."

Before Roman could tell his boss that he was fine, his legs gave way and his knees hit the floor with enough force for him to feel it in his teeth. He tried to get himself up, not wanting to be considered weak around the vampires, even as

Malakai forced him to sit down on the cold floor and lean against the cupboard.

Then Jasmine handed him some orange juice, and he drank it like it was the best drink he had ever had in his life. Exhaustion washed over him, a growl in his throat at being vulnerable, as Malakai glanced from him to his sister.

"You have not slept in weeks, and now that stubbornness is catching up with you. Sleep now, Roman. She will still be here when you awaken."

The she in question snorted, rolling her eyes as Malakai told him to sleep once more, with a little bit more conviction in his tone, his vampire compulsion slipping through the walls Roman had built up his in mind, now too tired to fight it even as he did.

He heard Malakai say something to Jasmine in a language he didn't know, then Jasmine was crouching down in front of him.

"It's all right, mutt. I'll be here when you come round. I swear it."

Both man and wolf were satisfied as Roman's head lolled forward and he welcomed the abyss.

CHAPTER THREE

Jasmine

JASMINE GLANCED AT THE UNCONSCIOUS WOLF, FROWNING EVEN as she held back on the urge to lick her lips to get another taste of him. She also tried not to think of his hardness pressed up against her, the warmth of his breath and skin. None of her other partners had gotten under her skin the way Roman Lowe did.

Rising up from the ground, she met Malakai's gaze, the barest hint of a smile on his lips. Those lips opened as if to speak, but Jasmine cut him off.

"Not a single word, Kai."

That only made her brother's tug of lips turn into a full-blown grin that made Jasmine want to deck him. She rolled her eyes hard and then thought of something that would quickly change the subject.

"How could you idiots have let him get close to Scarlett?"

The smile that had been on Malakai's lips faded as his gaze narrowed, and Jasmine regretted her snarky tone immediately, but the fact remained that they had let it happen.

"We did not expect him to be able to walk so easily in the evening, when the sun had barely gone down. And yes, the girls were delayed, having meant to be long out of the city when the vampire happened upon Scarlett. I would ask that you not mention this in front of Keeva. She has been beside herself since it happened."

An expression passed over Malakai's features, and then he

said, "Jazz, we never spoke of the incident to you when you were unconscious for fear it would upset you. How did you know?"

Jasmine strode around the counter, fighting the urge to look back at the sleeping wolf, and went to stand at the window. She looked out over Cork City, the place they had called home for more than a hundred years. Jasmine had witnessed the city burning in 1920, the deaths of countless freedom fighters, and more since claiming Cork as their own. Now the city was a vibrant hub for tech companies and nightlife. The Inferna had been in Ireland since the dawn of time, but Jasmine felt a special kinship to the city.

A pinprick of a headache, the only indication that a vision was trying to gently let her know it was on the horizon, made her sigh as she folded her arms across her chest and replied to Malakai, who had silently come to stand beside her.

"He came to visit me before I figured out how to get out of the spell. He told me how he had already gotten close to Scarlett and that he could have gutted her right there and then. He claimed the banshee could not have stopped him, and then he said that the obscurum could not stop him before he cut the child from the succubus. I'm still trying to figure out what he meant by calling Zeke obscurum."

"Did you see his face, Jazz? Do you know who he is?"

Jasmine shook her head at the panicked and slightly elevated tone of her brother. "Nada. He was so drenched in magic that he was nothing more than a shadow. It had a particular feel to it, so I might be able to recognise it again."

Malakai dragged his fingers through his hair. "How did you get out?"

"He had me trapped in the clearing. A never-ending loop that I couldn't free myself from. It was only when you said the only way is through that I copped myself on and went, like, duh. So I jumped into the fire and burnt myself out of the spell."

"Fucking hell, Jazz!"

Jasmine shrugged as she offered Malakai a smirk. "It was your idea, dear brother. I only followed what you told me to do."

Malakai nudged her shoulder with his own. "I guess we should let the other miscreants know that you are awake. There were a lot of people worried for you."

Himself included if the sadness in his eyes was anything to go by, but Jasmine didn't say anything to him about it. Gods, she was exhausted. All she wanted was a shower, clean clothes, and a stiff drink, but she wasn't sure that she could deal with everyone at once.

"You mind if we just let them sleep? I could use some time to readjust."

Malakai studied her for a moment, then nodded. "You know that as soon as Dylan wakes, he will go check on you and lose his mind if you are suddenly not there. He ..." Malakai trailed off as if he searched for the right words to convey his sentiment. "He has not been himself in a while."

"I'm not planning on running off anytime soon, and I will deal with Dylan."

"Without you, they will not see me coming. The empath is next for the slaughter."

The words of their enemy rattled around in her head as Jasmine headed toward the elevator. "I'm supposed to be here, Kai. But he threatened Dylan next. He knows enough about us to know about my powers. To know that Dylan is an empath. What the hell else does he know?"

Jasmine pressed the button as Malakai turned to her and inclined his head toward the kitchen.

"Are you not forgetting your wolf?"

With a snort, Jasmine rolled her eyes, brushing her hair off her shoulder. "You hired the mutt, Kai. And he is not my wolf. Not now, not ever."

The corners of Malakai's mouth tugged upward as

Jasmine snarled and stepped into the now open elevator and pressed the button for her floor. She heard the wolf groan as the doors closed, and Jasmine stepped back and rested her head against the metal.

Her thoughts drifted to Roman and their first interaction, when she had stood at the door of Malakai's office and called him Fido. Even most vampires were thrown when she went full ballbuster, unable to reconcile the sunny good looks with a no-nonsense attitude. Duke had quickly tried to rid her of that during their two-year relationship, telling her it was unbecoming for a vampire of her stature to use foul language or to talk back.

Jasmine had been so focused on defying destiny that she had not seen the signs of what Duke was doing until Dylan came to her and, after apologising for reading her, explained that her ex was making her miserable and it was breaking his heart to watch her wither like this, her spark going out.

Jasmine had dismissed Dylan, yet when Duke rubbished the idea of the family opening Dante's and Jazz working there, she knew he had been right. Duke was not the vampire for her.

But Roman hadn't balked at her rudeness. Instead he seemed to thoroughly enjoy the verbal sparring sessions between them.

Jasmine stepped out onto her floor and headed straight for the shower, her mind still thinking about that first interaction.

"I assume the only days you have issues with working, day or night, are around the full moon?"

"Kai." Jasmine had smirked. *"Fido could still work. We just need to get him a collar and a leash."*

Malakai had shot his sister a horrified look and went to apologize when he noticed the wolf grinning. "Darling, I would gladly wear a collar and leash if that's what you're into."

Her brother chuckled as Jazz sat back with a hiss at the innuendo. She folded her arms across her chest and ground her teeth together. Her brother and the wolf talked some nonsense for a few minutes as Jasmine studied him, this stupidly handsome man who was the opposite of everything she had pictured for her mate. He was rugged instead of clean-cut; his shoulder-length brown hair appeared the wolf had just run his fingers through it, and Jasmine wanted to do the same.

His stubble looked harsh around full lips, which made Jasmine wonder how it would feel against her skin. Dark brown eyes studied her with an intelligence that surprised her.

Malakai and the wolf were getting to their feet when Jasmine heard herself blurt out, "I still have a few questions."

"Shoot," Roman said as he settled back into his chair with a grin.

"Are you microchipped? All dogs in Ireland are required to wear a chip for tracking from their owners."

"I have the chip number at home on my official papers from the vet's. I'll bring it with me Saturday."

A little thrill of delight coursed through her even as she tried to mask her expression.

"When was the last time you were treated for fleas?"

Roman's grin made his entire face light up as he shot back at every question Jasmine threw at him.

"I'm up to date with all my inoculations, including kennel cough."

Jasmine had been frustrated at the attraction she felt toward the wolf, remembering the premonition about a wolf that would be her undoing or her awakening. She couldn't risk the former. She liked being undead. She didn't want to end up *dead* dead.

Shaking her head, she stripped and then stepped under the spray of the shower and rinsed off, trying to feel clean after her seven months of sleeping. She didn't linger in the shower, just washed her hair and then towelled it up so it would dry naturally. Jasmine dried off the rest of her and then dressed in skin-tight jeans and a pink Barbie top. She slipped her feet into her much-loved boots and then sat on the edge of the bed; the headache that was building now beat like a drum in her skull.

Jasmine closed her eyes and opened herself up to the vision, feeling her eyes roll behind her lids.

Then she was standing in the middle of Parnell Bridge in the city. Ash and dust fell all around her, the scent of burning saturating the air as humans and Inferna alike screamed. Winged creatures soared through the air, their claws as sharp as daggers and their teeth ripping through flesh and bone. Their screeches hurt her ears.

Jasmine looked down at her hands to see them coated in blood. She heard the sound of her name, jerking her head up to see Dylan pinned by something out of a horror movie, as the shadowy figure raised a thick gold stake into the air and then drove it into the heart of her brother.

Jasmine screamed a pained sound and her chest ached as Dylan, her vibrant and lovable rogue of a brother, burned to ash right in front of her. The ground shook as the city crumbled, and Jasmine heard herself mumble.

"The heart of the empath is fragile. War of hearts to tip the scales. If the seer and the empath meet face-to-face before the seventh night after she awakens, then his death is written in stone."

Jasmine's eyes darted open, panic in her chest as she pushed off the bed and went to get a bag, proceeding to shove some clothes into the bag. If Dylan woke early and came to see her, then he would die. Tears filled her eyes as she felt the panic well in her chest, unable to stop the fear that iced her veins.

Jasmine had ignored a warning a long time ago and they had lost Dante. It was her biggest regret, and it was all because Jasmine had thought she could skirt the visions. So she had defied the warnings, ignored that one of her blooded brothers would die if she did not heed the signs, and Dante's life had been sacrificed because of her.

She would not lose another brother.

She wouldn't survive it.

There were not many people in Cork who didn't know who she was, being the sister and one of the owners of two of Cork's most infamous companies, as well as a human influencer in her own way. Jasmine couldn't stay hidden from her brothers for long.

Seven days is all I need. I've waited seven months to hug him. I can wait seven more days.

Jasmine grabbed her purse and shoved it into her bag as she grabbed the keys to her car. The sun had not yet set, but she couldn't risk running into Dylan. She was in the elevator and heading downward a second later, trying to figure out where she was gonna go.

The doors opened, revealing the underground car park, and as soon as Jasmine stepped out and laid eyes on her yellow Mini Cooper, she grinned. She loved that car. Not only was it a typical girl car that would make people roll their eyes and instantly dismiss her, but she had made sure the car was car movie show-worthy, speedy and zany.

Jasmine crossed the empty car park, passing Kai's matte-black Aston Martin, Keeva's brand-new Golf, Zeke's Mercedes, and Dylan's cherry-red Ferrari Spider. There was a black BMW X5 at the end of the row that was not a car Jasmine was familiar with, but she assumed it was Roman's. It certainly looked like something Roman would drive.

Pressing the key to unlock her car, Jasmine had a second to sense that someone was behind her before she dropped the bag, and slipping the key between her fingers, she spun round, already punching with her fist.

The person that had snuck up on her growled, a familiar sound as she stomped down with her foot, earning a hiss for her troubles. Then Roman grabbed her wrist to halt her.

Jasmine glared at the wolf, and he let her go. "Is that how you get your rocks off, sneaking up on defenceless women?"

Roman's brown eyes narrowed as he replied, with no hint of the flash of anger in his eyes. "You are far from defenceless, Jasmine Cavanagh. Far from fucking defenceless."

They continued to glare at each other, the air becoming heated as Jasmine flicked her hair off her shoulders. "Well, this is nice and all, mutt. But I have to go. So, like, bye."

"Jasmine, the family will lose their shit if you just up and vanish without a reason. And where will you go? In case you'd forgotten, it's kinda the family side business to find those who don't want to be found."

Jasmine growled in frustration. "If Dylan and me lay eyes on one another in the next seven days, he will die, Roman. As in for real, die. I need to get out of here. So instead of stating the bloody obvious, unless you have a bright idea, then I'm out of here."

"I have somewhere you can go."

Jasmine studied the wolf's solemn expression, then sighed in resignation. "Okay, sure. Give me the address, and you can be on your way."

Roman flashed her what could only be described as a wolfish grin, and it made her want to sucker-punch him in his stupid, perfectly chiselled face.

"No can do. You would never find it. We go together."

Jasmine was already shaking her head before he finished speaking. "Nope, nada, never gonna happen. I think I'd rather still be asleep than have to spend seven days and nights with you."

"I promise not to bite unless you ask me to."

The wolf's tone was all husky and seductive, even as Jasmine felt her skin heat, now that she was chock-full of delicious wolf blood. She knew that he wouldn't let her go off on her own, even if she was fully capable of wiping the floor with him. She was, after all, a former shieldmaiden.

This is the path you must take.

There came a whisper in her mind and a certainty in her veins that she had to go with Roman, even if it was the last thing that she wanted to do out of fear that she would do something stupid like try and kiss him again. That little lapse had not curbed the visceral need in her, only ignited the flames.

Stepping back, Jasmine angled her body toward the car and slumped her shoulder. "Seems like I'm being told going with you is the right thing to do. So please don't drool on my seats."

Roman eyed the compact Mini as she walked round to the driver's side. "Jazz, we go in my car. It's tinted against the sun too. I ain't gonna fit in that thing."

Jasmine pointed a finger at Roman. "Bumblebee is not a thing."

"You named your car after a bee?"

His tone was amused, mocking even, as Jasmine snapped, "No, I named it after my favourite transformer. Now get in the car, or I go it alone."

Roman opened the car door as Jasmine picked up her bag and almost burst out laughing as Roman tried and failed to make his six foot of height and wide shoulders fit in the car. Then Jasmine considered that with Roman taking up so much space in her car, there was no way they wouldn't touch at some point, and she was not about to let that happen.

Grabbing his arm, Jasmine held on for a second before she dropped her hand. "Oh for fuck sake. Stop before you hurt yourself or, more importantly, Bumblebee."

She patted the bonnet of her car and stormed over to the BMW, climbing in when Roman opened the door for her. Roman got in beside her, pressing the button to start the car, and hard rock sounded from the speakers. Jasmine reached for the dial, then snatched her hand back.

"It's all right, darling, you're a DJ. You can play with my buttons."

Jasmine slumped in her seat with a grunt, ignoring the wolf, who was definitely pressing all the right buttons and was playing for keeps with every single word he said. So Jasmine decided she wanted to ruffle his feathers, and she leaned forward, scrolled through the collection of songs, and selected the very best of The Pussycat Dolls.

If the way he clenched his teeth together was anything to go by, score one point for Jasmine.

And when you tangled with werewolves, you took every cheap shot you could.

CHAPTER FOUR

Roman

THIS WAS A COLOSSALLY BAD IDEA.

Roman found himself repeating the mantra over and over again, as if somehow that would convince him to pull the car over to the side and call Malakai to come and collect the vampire who was so close to him that his inner wolf was clawing at his insides to get a piece of her.

He caught Jasmine looking at him every time he swallowed down a wince, but she made no comment. In fact, Jasmine had said little since poisoning his ears with Pussycat Dolls. She just kicked off her boots and leaned back into the seat, resting her feet on the dashboard. He wanted to tell her that that was a sure-fire way to break her legs if they crashed, yet he felt that she would no doubt reply with something about how if he wasn't a bad driver, then they wouldn't crash.

Roman kept his eyes on the road and drove out of the city, as if he were heading toward Cobh, then he veered off to the right and drove down a long and winding country road, one that most Irish would only refer to as a country road if a stripe of grass had grown up the centre. From the corner of his eye, he could see Jasmine taking it all in as the road disappeared and they delved deeper into a forest as the screen on his car indicated an incoming call with Malakai's name on the screen.

Jasmine leaned forward and pressed answer. "This is

Roman's phone. Sorry, he can't take your call right now as he is too busy being a pain in my ass. If you'd like to leave a message, please do so after the tone. BEEP!"

Roman felt his lips twitch as he tried not to laugh as his boss replied in a stern, very fatherly tone. "I assume you have a reasonable explanation for ghosting us and leaving the most secure building in the world when we are under attack."

It was a statement rather than a question, one that Jasmine had to answer.

"Look, Kai, I'm sorry I did a runner, but Dylan's life is in danger. I saw it."

"Understood. You check in with me nightly, or I will come looking for you."

Jasmine rolled her eyes. "Okay, *Mom*. Jesus, Kai, you are such a helicopter parent."

"Roman?" It looked like Malakai was done dealing with Jasmine and was now focused on him.

"Yes, sir?"

There was a slight pause, as if his boss was trying to think of the way to word what he wanted to say, something Roman had seen him do numerous times, and then Malakai spoke. "She does not leave your side."

"Yes, sir."

"How long, Jazz?" Malakai asked. His tone held a vicious edge to it.

"A week. I can come home in a week," she confirmed to Malakai, and Roman knew that she hadn't lied to him about her visions. She had trusted him with knowing about her gift.

"I will expect you both then. And Jazz?"

"Yeah?" the vampire beside him sighed.

"Play nice."

Then Malakai hung up before Jazz could bark out an answer, and from the way she spluttered, she had one poised to shoot back at her brother. She glanced at him, ready to take aim with her words, when the phone rang again, this time with an unknown number on the display.

Roman let it ring out, but then it started up again immediately. Roman growled and pressed answer on his steering wheel.

"Lowe."

"Wow, who has pissed you off to have you in full alpha snarl this evening, honey?"

Roman stole a quick glance at Jasmine, reining in the smug satisfaction at the fact that she had bristled as soon as the voice on the phone had called him honey. She had this pissed-off look on her face that made him think she was jealous, and he would take it.

"First Con calling me baby and now you with honey? Is your marriage so dull you have to call up your single friends and tease them?"

Abbie laughed down the phone. "You know how this works, Roman. Conor calls first 'cause he can talk you into anything, then they send me to make sure that you know I would hunt you down with my fave rifle if you missed a family celebration. Or would you prefer if I get Tanaka to call you?"

"Hell no," he barked out, turning down another dirt trail, edging the sturdy car off-road and into the forest. "You know you're my favourite, Abigail."

He knew his voice had dropped slightly as he grinned, feeling the heat of Jazz's gaze on him.

"That tone doesn't work on me, buddy. You tried that every time you brought my mate home rapturously drunk. And remember I can still kick your ass even if I am an old woman."

It was Roman's turn to laugh. "Old woman, my ass. Come on now, Abs, why the mountain of calls?"

Abbie sighed, and she took a sip of something she was drinking. "Conor said you sounded tired and he was worried about you. This call is to reassure your work wife that you are squared away."

"I promise I am. I had a nap this afternoon and plan to sleep away the next few hours. I will see you Friday, and the idiot can see I'm fine."

Shit, Friday was only three days away. And he couldn't leave Jasmine by herself, so he would just have to bring her with him. It looked like Jasmine was doing the math herself, her eyes filling with curiosity as Roman said to Abbie, "Abbie, sweetheart. I'll see you all Friday. Can you let the guys know I'll be bringing a plus-one?"

"Roman Aloysius Lowe! Are you finally bringing a girl home to meet the parents? Or is it a guy? You spill the beans right now, mister!"

"See ya Friday, Abbie. Go annoy your mate."

Roman disconnected the call, cutting Abbie off as she continued speaking, and glanced at Jasmine.

"Well, that was rude, Aloysius."

"It's only Abbie. She's used to it."

Jasmine just hmmmed and cast her eyes out into the darkness that had quickly descended. Roman kept going through Marlogue Woods until his cabin came into view, right on the edge of the water. Jasmine leaned forward in her seat, her eyes wide.

She was probably used to all the luxuries of life, and he had brought her to his home, where he had brought no other person besides his little family. He wondered if she would be disgusted at his little escape from the city, but then she peered over at him and said, "Oh my god, this is amazing."

Jasmine was out the door before he had stopped the car, striding across the drive in her bare feet. She skipped down the pathway and dipped her toes in the water, letting loose a squeal of pure joy as the waves lapped at her feet, which made Roman want to stalk right on up to her and kiss her hard.

When she turned around to look at him with the first genuine smile she had ever graced him with, his foolish heart skipped a beat and something strange welled in his chest. Pushing down every claiming instinct in him, Roman grabbed Jasmine's bag from the car and left her to her little peace while still leaving the door open so he could see her.

His cabin was rustic, but it was his. Growing up, Roman had nothing, no family, no proper home, no real identity. It had taken him leaving the pack behind for him to find his place in the world, and one of the first things he had done was to acquire this piece of land, and he had built the cabin by hand.

It had a kitchen-come-living area, with a table just big enough for two. He had a bigger table in the storage room for when the gang came over, and they usually sat outside, come hail, rain, or snow. He had three bedrooms: his own, the one usually taken up by Conor and Abbie, and the last bedroom, where the others crashed.

He was too far out for proper electricity, so he had installed a generator. Roman fired that up, then took a couple of mugs from the cupboard to make some coffee when he felt Jazz come to stand in the doorway, but she did not cross the threshold.

He raised his brows. "Vampires don't need permission to enter someone's home."

"But it's rude to go where you haven't been invited."

That surprised him, because he also always waited on an invitation before entering someone's house. He leaned against the archway that separated the kitchen from the living room and motioned with his hand.

"I wouldn't have brought you here if you weren't welcome. But if you want an invitation, I'm afraid I'm all out of glitter," he announced to her as he angled his body as if he was going back into the kitchen area.

Jasmine rolled her eyes as she stepped inside his home and then muttered, "Idiot."

Her terms of endearment for him were just heart-warming.

Roman made them each a coffee, adding in a little spoon of sugar he knew she liked, and then strode out to see her wandering around, picking up pictures and trinkets and studying them. She held up a picture of him and Conor, dressed in fatigues, grinning like idiots in some bar in the US. It was one Abbie had taken on the day Conor had asked him to be his best man.

"This is Conor, right?" Jasmine asked, scrutinizing the picture like she was trying to remember every aspect of it.

"Sure is. We've been friends for about sixty years now."

Jasmine was still looking at the picture, then she said with a wistful tone, "He's like your chosen brother."

Roman chuckled as he walked around the couch and set the mugs on the hand-carved coffee table. "I don't know if I would have chosen him, but he is. When Conor was first assigned to my team, he was this cocky SOB who just wouldn't quit. But he had an iron will and unbreakable loyalty. He saved my life. He is my brother."

Jasmine set the picture down, grabbed her coffee, and stood by the fireplace as Roman took a seat on the sofa. Then Jasmine smiled. "Zeke is like that. Although he didn't have much of a choice at accepting us as family. I'm very good at persuading people."

Jasmine ran her fingers over the fireplace, her fingers halting at the bullets that lined the fireplace. "Mementos?"

"One for every time they fished a bullet from me." Roman tapped his shoulder. "And one they couldn't fish out before my skin healed over it."

Jasmine pursed her lips and regarded him in a way he couldn't decipher. "I like this place. It's quiet. Peaceful. It reminds me of the home I had when I was human."

"Took us a few weeks to build it. Then I made the furniture one summer when we weren't deployed."

"You did not make all this by hand," Jasmine accused him as she sank down onto one of the fireside chairs.

"I did. I'm very good with my hands." He grinned over at her, chest swelling as she narrowed her gaze, tensed, and he heard her mumble, "Oh, I bet you are."

"The windows are shuttered, so I'll close them all during the day," he told her, changing the subject, watching as she relaxed and took a sip from her coffee.

"You would think that after seven months trapped inside my body that I would never want to sleep again, but I do feel tired. I'll sleep when the sun rises, though, 'cause there is only so much I can do to entertain myself during the daylight with no TV."

Roman said nothing as he watched her curl her legs up under herself and smile. Then she realized that he was watching her, and she quirked an eyebrow. "What?"

"It seems I misjudged you. I was afraid my modest home would not be somewhere you would feel comfortable, yet I don't think I've ever seen you this chill."

Jasmine switched her mug from one hand to another. "I might like nice things, but we didn't always have them. We were poor, like dirt poor. I remember a time when all we had was the clothes on our backs. It was a time when the Inferna frowned upon vampires because we were made not born, and vampires couldn't sit on the council. We had nothing. But Malakai put a stop to that. He got his hands dirty, and we never forget where we came from."

"Working closely with him over the past couple of months means I can honestly say Malakai is one of those rare people, rare Inferna, who doesn't think he is better than everyone else. Most people would hear about my affliction and pity me. Malakai doesn't. He didn't shun me like most would."

Jasmine reached out and set her mug down on the table.

"Malakai has a way of seeing the best qualities in people and making sure they are utilized. But he used to put everyone before himself, so I'm glad he has Keeva. She is so the opposite of Malakai, yet they work."

Keeva Cross was a banshee who was known as Death because of her ability to kill with her touch. Up until recently, everyone, including herself, had thought she couldn't even scream like other banshees, but she had found her voice it just wasn't the predicting death kind of scream. Yes , her scream was powerful, but it was her touch that embodied death completely, causing not predicting the kill. Keeva was a flame-haired, down-to-earth, no-agenda type of girl who Roman would have recruited to his team years ago if he had known she existed.

They had worked the bar a few nights together over the past couple of months, and the Inferna was easy to laugh, quick to dispel trouble, and she had no airs or graces. Despite the fact she had married one of the richest men in the world, she still wore beat-up Converse and cleaned up messes with the rest of them.

Keeva was good people.

"So where are we going Friday night?" Jasmine asked as she leaned her head against the back of the chair.

Roman rolled his shoulders, draining his own mug, then answered Jasmine. "It's one of the team's birthdays. We never miss one. It won't be a fancy affair. Just meeting at our spot for a few drinks. I apologize in advance for all the questions you will no doubt be bombarded with."

"And you've never brought someone to meet them?"

"Never."

"I could stay here. I mean, like, you don't have to bring me."

Roman heard something in her tone he didn't like, as if she had been left behind before and it had bothered her. Jasmine Cavanagh was confidence in a tall, leggy, gorgeous package, and to hear the insecurity in her voice made the wolf in his mind snarl, flashing its teeth and growling, wanting to make whoever had hurt her bleed.

"If I didn't want to bring you, Jasmine, then I would have made an excuse and not gone. I want you to come. Read into that what you want."

She glanced away from him for second before she peered over at him, and he saw the faint outline of red in her irises. Then she got this devilish look on her face as she got to her feet.

"I think I might go for a swim," the vampire declared as she strode out the door, pulling her hair into a ponytail. Roman followed her to the door, then down the path until she stood at the water's edge like before, dipping her toes in.

"Did you bring a suit?" His brain was a little scrambled at the thought of seeing Jasmine in a swimsuit, but nothing prepared him for the playful vampire in front of him.

Jasmine shrugged, the ghost of a smile on her lips as she winked at him over her shoulder. "It's only us. Who cares if I have a suit or not?"

Then to punctuate her question, Jasmine pulled her pink tee over her head and tossed it to the side, and before Roman could drag his eyes away from the creamy skin that he ached to touch, Jasmine stood in just a pink bra and matching panties that made his mouth water.

Runes were tattooed all along her spine, from neck to ass, and Roman knew he had to get out of here before he forgot that she didn't really want him; she just wanted to banish the visions from her mind.

The minx strode straight into the water until it was up to her waist, and then she dived under, the water rippling as she swam a little way out as Roman's keen eyesight kept track of her. Her head broke through the water, and under the moonlight, shadows danced along her skin. She looked like a siren trying to lure him into murky waters.

Jasmine had always been beautiful, but tonight she looked ethereal, as if the moon itself had created her, and now, like him, it was unable to drag its gaze from her as she ran her hands over her face and hair, grinning at him. She splashed about, then with a grin that looked more wolf than vampire, she beckoned him to her, and he stepped forward.

Both man and wolf were in agreement that they would have Jasmine Cavanagh and she would want him as much as he wanted her. Her eyes flashed white, and then she laughed, diving back under the water as Roman tried to rein in his libido.

Jasmine was trouble with a capital *T*, and there was no way Roman was getting out of the way when trouble came for him.

Hell, he didn't even want to.

Yup, the big bad werewolf was in trouble.

CHAPTER FIVE

Jasmine

PANIC WELLED INSIDE HER AS SHE DARTED THROUGH THE FOREST, *her muscles burning, and she knew if she still had to breathe, her lungs would have been on fire. Her brothers, Malakai and Dylan, kept pace beside her as Jasmine scanned her eyes back and forth, hoping, praying that she had not been the one who would have sealed her brother's fate by ignoring the path chosen by the gods.*

She stumbled over her own footing as images of Dante plagued her, his screams of agony shredding her non-beating heart as she urged her other brothers forward.

I have been selfish, and in finding one brother, I have condemned another. *She had seen visions of their future brother, Ezekiel, for years now, and she had fought against her curiosity to go and see him for herself. The voices in her head had whispered to her, telling her that it was not time yet to go to Ezekiel, but Jasmine had defied them, thinking she knew better than beings who had gifted her with visions of other people's destiny from when she was a young child.*

And when she defied them, it had sent a ripple along her own future, and now, after bearing witness to the torment and torture of their oldest brother, Dante, her and Malakai's blooded brother, Jasmine had been filled with dread.

They had been told that Dante had been captured by a rival Kiss, and she could still smell the scent of the fire and the burnt flesh as she offered herself up to the gods in place of her brother.

Time seemed to stall on its axis, the world around them frozen as Jasmine came face-to-face with a cloaked figure who clutched a staff and looked at her with skeletal features and eyes as white as a dove.

"You have dismissed the gift we have bestowed upon you. You have thought yourself a better judge than we."

Jasmine dropped to one knee, bowing her head. "I was foolish, weak. I implore you to punish me and not Dante for my actions."

"It serves us not to punish you. Losing your brother and living with your actions will be punishment enough. We need you as you are … the other is merely collateral damage."

Time sped up once more, and then she was moving, suddenly on her feet, tears running down her face as they stumbled into the home where they once were born and Jasmine let loose a strangled sob as she caught sight of Dante's sword in the dirt, his cloak still smouldering as ash fluttered about in the wind.

Jasmine fell to her knees, her palms resting on the burnt edges of Dante's cloak. "This is all my fault. I have caused this."

Malakai rested his hand on her shoulder and squeezed. "You did not see this coming until it was already too late. If we were meant to save him, you would have envisioned it earlier. Dante chose the path he walked upon. His death is not your fault."

Jasmine wanted to scream at him that yes, it was her fault. She had started this, and had she not gone to see the teenager at the farm, then Dante would not be nothing more than dust or ash. They might not have agreed with Dante a lot of the time, but he was their brother, and as if it were Jasmine's own hand that had burned him, she felt the guilt of it like an anchor that threatened to drag her under the water.

They can never know the truth. I can never tell them I could have prevented this.

Jasmine woke with a gasp, sitting upright as she sensed the sun set and night beckoned her to it. She took a few minutes to collect herself, listening as Roman tried to be quiet, and she smelled the breakfast he was cooking. He had been a surprisingly good housemate even after she had lost her mind and gone almost skinny-dipping in the water.

But she had never felt so free, as if the guilt she had been carrying for centuries was gone, and then her nightmare had reminded her of what she had done, the secret she had managed to keep hidden from Malakai and Dylan, not even sharing it with Zeke once he became her confidant.

As she had swum under the moonlight, Roman had done nothing but sit down, his watchful eyes on her at all times, and even though she could scent the lust rolling off him, he acted the perfect gentleman, much to her frustration.

Was it really bad that she wanted to unnerve him, the wolf who didn't seem to be fazed by much, who didn't so much as flinch as she threw insults at him?

An image of Dante's ashes filled her mind as she heard Roman tap on the door and tell her breakfast was ready. Jasmine slipped out of bed, wearing an old tee that once belonged to Dylan, that hit just to her knees. They were the same height, she and Dylan, but she was a slighter build, so it kinda fell longer than it would on him.

Jasmine didn't bother to tidy herself up as she yanked open the door and strode to the kitchen area, sitting down and inhaling the scent of coffee as she yawned.

"Good evening to you too, sunshine."

Jasmine growled as she took a large gulp of coffee, then replied. "Coffee first—stupid everything else after. I don't speak to wolves who have been awake since gods knows when without coffee. Even if he does make a half-decent breakfast."

"I think that has got to be the nicest thing you've ever said to me." Roman grinned annoyingly cheerfully at her.

"Don't let it go to your head, wolf. I don't make much sense until after I've had coffee."

Roman chuckled, and Jasmine slyly ran her eyes over him

as she drank her nectar of the gods. Today he wore army shorts and a plain black tee that stretched across his chest. He had a slender waist, but she knew he had muscular thighs, and she could see the strength in his calves.

Over the past day or so, Jasmine had been surprised at how easy it was to spend time with Roman. He had taken her on a run through the forest. They'd played cards, and Jasmine was surprised when he didn't let her win. He'd shown her his small but unique collection of books, and she had lounged outside of the house while he had fixed a loose leg on one of the chairs.

It was so blissfully normal that it made her consider not going back when the seven days were over.

"Eat up before it gets cold. We need to head out in a bit."

Oh, that was a new development to Jasmine, and she leaned forward to rest her elbows on the table. "Where are we going?"

"For supplies. For a vampire, you eat a hell of a lot of food."

Jasmine rolled her eyes, something she seemed to do a lot around Roman. "Speaking of, I'm gonna need to get blood. If you drop me off somewhere, I can grab a quick bite and be back before you know it."

It was Roman's turn to roll his eyes then. "Nice try. Not happening. And you have blood on tap here. You don't need to go in search of a meal."

"Dude, I've just gotten the taste out of my mouth. I do not need another reminder of what dogs taste like. Makes me feel like I'm eating a puppy."

A muscle in Roman's jaw ticked, and it was the first time something she said had angered him, but his face remained impassive. If this was any of her exes, they would have made some sort of remark, yet Roman kept his opinion to himself.

"Are you sure?" Jasmine prompted. "Last time you passed out."

"Last time I had just run until my legs wanted to fall off, had not slept in seventy-two hours, and skipped dinner. This time I've got a full stomach, and I slept like a log last night."

Jasmine scented the lie in his words, knew he had stayed awake to make sure she hadn't tried to slip out or to protect her, and when he had slept, it was lightly and he would wake like a shot at the slightest strange noise.

Roman bit into some toast and then sat back in his chair, as if he was letting Jasmine make the decision for herself. She was reluctant to feed from him again because it would no doubt ignite the spark between them, but she knew deep down feeding from him was exactly what she wanted.

She ate some more of her food, drank a little more coffee, and then stood with a pained sigh. She walked over to where Roman sat and pointed to his arm. He tilted his head to the side as if teasing her. Jasmine's eyes latched onto the pulse at his neck before she used every ounce of self-restraint to drag her eyes back to his face, wanting to punch the bastard for his smugness.

Her fangs elongated as Roman lifted up his arm. The veins in his wrist pulsed, and she lowered her lips to his skin, licking over the flesh, shivering when Roman shuddered. She pierced his skin as gently as she could, then swallowed hard, unable to hold back her moan. She bit down a little harder as Roman barked out a husky curse.

Suddenly, he shifted her so that she was riding his thigh, not caring that the only barrier between her core and his skin were her panties and his shorts. His free hand wrapped around her waist, pressing her down more, and they both groaned as Jasmine took one more swallow, retracted her fangs and licked over the puncture wounds to seal the broken skin.

She lifted her head to look into eyes that were wolf amber, and Jasmine had a second to think before Roman snarled and muttered, "Fuck it."

His mouth captured hers a second later, devouring her with hungry lips, nipping at her bottom lip so she opened her mouth, and then he was tasting her, licking into her mouth like she had licked his skin, and then Jasmine kissed him back, her arms going around his neck as she rocked against his thigh.

Roman growled his appreciation as he continued to kiss her with a relentless pace, hands sliding up to cup her ribs just so that his fingers grazed the underneath of her aching breasts.

The wolf pulled back, his eyes still amber, his chest heaving as he snarled. Jasmine took advantage of their position to run her fingers through his hair, igniting the heat in his gaze.

"For fuck sake. I didn't plan to kiss you. Not when we really need to leave soon or we will be late. I want to take my time with you."

He leaned in and rubbed his harsh stubble against her chin. Jasmine flushed as she clambered off him, shaking her head as she retreated.

"That will not be happening again," Jasmine said with little conviction in her words as Roman got to his feet, stalking toward her.

"It is. You and I both know it. I would finish what we just started if I had more time, but if I do not get somewhere by a certain time, there will be a bounty on my head."

Jasmine spun on her heel and escaped into the bedroom, locking the door and leaning against it as she tried to halt the delicious images from her mind. Shaking her head, Jasmine had a quick shower and changed into loose yoga pants and a tee that read, "Valhalla awaits."

When she had plucked up enough courage, she grabbed a hoodie and slipped it on, then she ventured outside after finding the cabin empty, but she spied Roman leaning against his chair. Jasmine walked around to the car and hopped in, not even glancing at Roman.

The wolf got in beside her and started the car, reversing around until he was driving back the way they came. They drove in silence, with Jasmine looking out the window as the forest passed her by. With each kilometre they edged closer to civilization, she felt more pinpricks of anxiety. She must have started tapping the window because suddenly Roman pulled the car over to the side, stopping.

"Okay, spill. What had you spooked?"

"I am not spooked," she snapped, even though Roman didn't deserve her anger.

He tapped his nose. "I might not be able to shift, but I am still a wolf. I can smell when your scent changes. So talk it out or we don't move."

Jasmine balled her hands into fists. "Okay, I don't like surprises. I always know what's going to happen so not knowing unnerves me. I'm scared we will run into Dylan or while I've been hiding away with you, my family has been in danger."

"Jazz, I check in with Malakai every day, sometimes numerous times. If something was wrong, he would tell me and I would take you back. I need you to trust me, so I'm not going to tell you where we are going. I need you to see that I can keep you safe. Can you deal with that?"

Jasmine frowned, surprised at the fact Roman had been in contact with her brother constantly. But she decided to trust him, so she nodded and turned her gaze back out into the wilderness.

Roman steered the car forward, and soon they travelled into Midleton town centre and into the almost empty car park next to the supermarket. There were plenty of spots, but Roman continued to cross the car park, pulling to a stop next to a secondhand Golf that made Jasmine smile.

She glanced at Roman. "We're meeting Keeva?"

"Not just Keeva."

A bulky frame stepped out of the shadows, and Jasmine squealed in delight. She muttered "thank you" to Roman before she dove out of the car and raced toward Zeke, throwing her arms around the vampire, who hugged her back with a fierceness that threatened to undo her.

Zeke had always been shrouded in darkness, a creature who never fully accepted what he was, but Scarlett, his reluctant succubus, had changed all that. He fed now, every day, and he had always been this imposing figure, but now, now Zeke looked like he could bench-press an elephant.

Zeke smoothed her hair off her face. "Are you okay?"

"I am. How's Scarlett and my niece?"

Zeke chuckled. "Scarlett is annoyed at my fussing. Your niece is almost ready to meet you."

Zeke lifted his almost black eyes to stare at Roman, then he focused on her. "Is the wolf treating you well?"

"He'd get a passable review on TripAdvisor."

Zeke smiled at her, one of those rare glimpses of who he was when not weighed down by darkness.

It is why you were drawn to him, because you carry your own darkness within you.

Jasmine ignored her thoughts as she turned to the petite woman who leaned against the Golf with hair the colour of flames and eyes as green as emeralds. Keeva Cross grinned at her, then strode over to her, stiffening when Jazz went to hug her, as if the realization that Jasmine was not affected by her death touch still shocked her.

Then she softened, giving Jasmine a quick squeeze before she walked around and took out a duffel bag, handing it to Roman, who opened up the back door of the car and put the bag inside.

"Just a few things to keep you going. Roman said you

might need some clothes. Don't worry, I didn't pack it. Scarlett is nesting, so we let her pick out some clothes. I have no clue what she packed, but it was either Scarlett or Kai, considering I know next to nothing about fashion."

Jasmine grinned at the banshee. "Still can't bring yourself to wear the dresses Malakai got you."

"I mean, one of them could pay for Grayce's college. It would not go well with Converse."

Jasmine laughed out loud, the ache in her chest from earlier dissipating as she hugged Keeva and Zeke once more before Zeke and Roman headed off for a little walk, going far enough that she couldn't hear them, the wolf nodding at whatever Zeke was saying.

"I mean, I'm normally oblivious to these sorts of things, but the sexual tension between you two is enough to feed Scarlett for weeks."

Jasmine glared at Keeva, who held up her hands in apology. "Hey, like I said, I could totally be reading this all wrong, but if I'm not, if you wanna get soldier boy naked, then you have another four days to get him out of your system before you two have to be around your brothers. Think about that."

Zeke and Roman came back then, stopping the conversation, and Jasmine waved them off and then turned to Roman, who was watching her cautiously. Jasmine crooked her finger at him, and when Roman lowered his head, she gave him a quick peck on the cheek, the warmth in his smile warming her skin.

"Thank you. I didn't realize how much I needed to see him."

"He's your brother. I get it. Now let's go get some food so that I can keep you fed. And if you are a good little vampire, I might even splurge and get some of that ridiculously expensive caramel ice cream you like."

Roman held out a hand toward her, then froze, as if he

hadn't meant to do it, and he made to pull his outstretched hand away. Jasmine didn't let herself think; she just slipped her fingers into his and, with a smile, pulled him toward the supermarket, telling him all the things he needed to buy, and when the wolf chuckled, Jasmine was sure butterflies fluttered in her stomach.

CHAPTER SIX

Roman

ROMAN WOKE UP TO THE SOUND OF SCREAMS. HE BOLTED upright, pulling his Glock from where it was behind the headboard. He was just about to get out of the bed when his bedroom door opened, spilling light into his bedroom, and Jasmine stood there, staring at him, her big blue eyes filled with terror.

"Bullets won't kill me," she remarked with that dry tone of hers, her voice sounding a little hoarse.

Roman didn't know what to say in response to that, so instead he said, "Nightmares?"

"Something like that."

And he understood in that moment, just like when Conor woke up screaming, clutching at his chest as if he had been shot over and over. It was like that vacant look Ezra got when he heard a power drill, having been captured on a previous mission. Hell, even Roman himself had triggers that set him off, whether it was the scent of rose perfume his mother used to wear or the occasional time a car backfiring sent him ducking for cover.

Jasmine had her own variation of PTSD to deal with.

Roman reached behind the bed and holstered the gun, then made room for Jasmine, her eyes widening when she realized what he was doing. She opened her mouth to speak. However, Roman cut her off.

"Close the door before you get in. You're letting the cold in."

He closed his eyes, wondering if she would run. Roman heard the door close, and he used all of his training to steady his heart rate as Jasmine lay down beside him. Neither of them said anything for a torturous amount of time, then Jasmine released an aggravated sigh and she shifted in the bed, letting Roman feel the weight of her eyes on him.

Slowly, cautiously, he opened his eyes to see Jasmine with her head on the pillow and her hands tucked under her chin. Her hair fell around her face and made her look almost human, but there was no doubt in Roman's mind that she was far from it.

"You're staring at me."

"My eyes were closed, darling. You were looking at me first."

She rolled her eyes, then closed them as if she meant to go back to sleep.

"If you tell anyone I willingly got into bed with you, I will make you bleed."

"I promise that anything that happens in this bed or this house is just between us," he said with a chuckle, yet Jasmine didn't respond, and for a moment, Roman feared she had slipped back into the unconscious state she had been in for almost seven months. Then Jasmine huffed out a sigh, curling herself closer to him.

Roman was in a state of hyperawareness, unable to fall back asleep, as Jasmine kept coming closer until she rested her head in the crook of his neck and placed a hand on his chest. Hell's bells, he wanted to touch her. He wanted to yank her flush against him, her body draped over his.

He kept his hands and thoughts to himself as the minutes ticked by slowly until Jasmine bolted upright, her eyes that terrifying white, and she reached out with her hand.

"The wolf is howling at the door with teeth and claws and

bone. From darkness comes light. One lie to divide them. One truth to set them free. The wolf in sheep's clothing, the traitor in our midst. Betrayal comes from the ones we least expect."

Jasmine blinked her eyes, and they slowly faded from white to blue as she glanced over her shoulder at Roman, who just lay there during the vision, ready to bite into a vein if she started haemorrhaging again.

"Did I go all creepy seer again?" she asked, brushing her hair from her face.

"A little. I'm kinda used to it now. It honestly freaked me the fuck out when you first did it. But now, it's just part of what makes you you."

Jasmine frowned at him as she pursed her lips together.

"What?" Roman asked, slightly amused.

"Nothing." Jasmine sighed, then shook her head. "You make it hard not to like you, furball."

That made Roman bark out a laugh, shaking his head as he sat up and leaned back against the headboard. "I take back what I said earlier. That's the nicest thing you've ever said to me."

Jasmine shook her head at him, but there was an unmistakable ghost of a smile on her lips. "Well, enough of the niceties. Ugh, like hell am I going to be able to sleep for the rest of the day. Now, so I don't make an ass of myself, tell me a little about your friends."

Roman folded his hands behind his head as Jasmine turned to face him, sitting like she was about to start meditating. Instead, she rested her elbows on her thighs and leaned her chin into her hands, waiting for him to speak.

"Well," Roman started, unable to stop himself from smiling. "You already know about Conor and Abbie. Then you have Tyler, who looks like he is about to break some bones, but honestly, he has the best heart of anyone I've known. Then Réiltín, she's like the brightest person I know with the ability to defuse any situation. Then there's Hiro—that dude never has a smile off his face—and finally there's Ezra."

As it always did when he thought of Ezra, his voice held an edge, and of course, Jasmine caught it. "You worry about him?"

"I worry about them all. But ya, Ezra the most. He was captured by a cartel a couple years back, and it's like he never really believes he made it out. He has a temper, which is always dangerous when you turn into a monster with claws and teeth."

He studied the blond vampire for a moment, his own wolf at the forefront of his mind as he watched her. It whined, swiping out with a paw, projecting its thoughts of wanting to be in fur so the seer could run her fingers through it.

Roman, who was well-schooled on how to keep his emotions and reactions in check, feared he had betrayed himself, especially when Jasmine leaned forward suddenly and tapped his forehead.

"Behave," was all she said, and the wolf flopped down on its belly, resting its muzzle on his front leg, angling its head slightly.

Jasmine pulled back her hand and grinned at Roman, who was perplexed at how she had known.

"I don't have to be a seer to know that you want to know how, right?"

"How did I give it away?"

"Silly furball," she replied with a snort. "You didn't. Most shifters are one and the same with their inner beast. It gives them this edgy aura. Yet that's doubled for you. I can scent the flash of aggression, and I can kinda pick up on the visual of a wolf in your mind."

"You a mind reader now as well?"

"Hell no." She laughed.

"Thank god," Roman muttered as Jasmine slipped off the bed and headed for the door. He watched her go, running his eyes over her backside and grinning when she glanced over her shoulder and frowned.

"Stop checking out my ass, wolf."

"Yes, ma'am," Roman ground out, keeping his eyes firmly planted on her ass. He heard her growl, then she vanished from the door with inhuman speed. Roman remained in the bed for a few minutes to try and hide the raging hard-on he was sporting, but as soon as he heard the water turn on, he saw images of Jasmine naked in the shower, rivulets of water dripping down her skin and body. Roman bolted for his own shower, turning the water to frigid cold in order to quell thoughts of just saying fuck it once more and finally, after months and months of dreaming, having the woman who drove him slightly insane.

Roman was dressed and sitting on the sofa an hour later as he waited for Jasmine to finish getting ready, listening to her sing, badly, along with some song she was playing on her phone. Roman was surprised that he had gotten quite used to having the vampire around in his space, his eyes snagging on her hoodie, the scent of wildflowers and sunshine mixed in with his own. They had four more days until she could go back to Sicarius Security, and if Roman stopped lying to himself, he wanted to keep her here.

Mate.

The wolf projected its thoughts to Roman, making it quite clear what it wanted. Roman had been a lone wolf long before he had joined the covert ops team, which on official paper was a navy seal posting but had been far from the normal army service he had signed up for. And then, he had mostly been a one-night-stand kinda fella, never considering that what Conor and Abbie had was meant for him.

But if Ezekiel Collins, the man who was once a ripper, unable to control his vampire nature and hunger, could fall for and be expecting a child with Scarlett Russell, the sweetest, kindest person and succubus you could meet, why couldn't he be happy?

"You are an abomination. A cancer within the pack. It is not natural for a shifter to be unable to change form. It is unacceptable for a wolf who carries the scent of a future alpha to be unable to fight as a wolf in a dominance battle. You are not my son. She must have rutted with some other degenerate behind my back."

His father's words came back to haunt him, the accusations thrown at him much like they had his mother. Roman's mother had borne the brunt of his father's anger. He'd demoted her to the bottom tier, the weakest, and she had become a plaything for the other male members of the pack. Her mind had fractured, and now, his mother was one of the wolves that had stayed in fur too long and had left behind their humanity.

Sometimes, when he dared to get close enough to pack lands, from the birthplace he had been banished from, he could hear her howl in the distance.

A growl rumbled in his chest, and he felt the urge to put his fist through a wall.

"Well, I am certainly not going anywhere with you in that pissed-off mood."

Roman slowly turned his head to see Jasmine standing in the archway, hands on her hips and eyebrows arched in a jaunty expression. Roman's anger quickly dissipated, replaced by another emotion as he roamed his eyes over Jasmine.

The blond vampire had left her hair down but managed to curl the ends so they bounced when she moved. Her curves were clad in leather-look pants, a white vest, and a leather jacket. She wore little or no makeup, because she certainly didn't need it. A coat of ruby-red lipstick made her lips look fuller, and Roman knew that he would not end the night without having a taste of her.

When Roman pushed off the couch, he realized her feet

were clad in black boots that had ankle-breaker heels. He glanced down at his own black jeans, worn work boots, plain black tee, and flannel shirt, and then back at Jasmine.

"I feel like I should change," he grunted out as Jasmine flicked her hair off her shoulders, a familiar thing she did whenever she was trying to mask whatever it was she was thinking, or when she was trying to throw her brothers off the scent of what she was feeling.

"No time for you to be insecure, Roman. These are your friends. I'm the one that's gate-crashing."

"It not gate-crashing if I want you there."

Their eyes clashed across the room, and Roman took an involuntary step toward Jasmine, the vampire's eyes darkening as they widened. However, she jerked her gaze away from his a second later and all but ran toward the door, the wolf inside him howling for him to go and chase her, and he had to leave her to get to the car and hop inside before he managed to get a grip on himself.

Roman had a feeling that tonight was going to be the biggest test of his control.

He wanted his hands on her curves, his tongue tasting her skin. His cock was rock-hard against the seam of his fly, and before Roman locked up and went outside, he tried to readjust himself to ease some of the pain, but nothing short of getting Jasmine naked was going to do that.

"You are a grown-ass man, not a horny teenager. Get a grip, Roman."

As he made his way toward the car, he was certain that Jasmine was laughing at him, but by the time he was behind the wheel, the vampire had such an innocent expression on her face that he just had to say something.

"Has anyone ever told you to not run from a wolf, lest they chase you?"

Something dark crossed over her face for the briefest of seconds, and then it was gone as Jasmine snorted and reached over and patted his head. "Who's a good little wolf? Is Romie a good little wolf? Yes, he is."

Roman snarled and snapped his teeth, but the smart-ass yanked her hand back, and as she leaned back into her seat, a smug smile curving her lips, she swung with another one of those hard hitters of hers. "You actually think you could catch me? Only if I let you, furball."

"Challenge accepted, bloodsucker."

Roman started the car and shifted into gear lest he pull Jasmine into his lap and have hot, dirty sex with her. They didn't speak again until they were on the main dual carriageway and Jasmine started humming the tune to Duran Duran's "Hungry Like the Wolf."

Roman was pretty sure she was trying to needle him and make him react, and while he was seconds away from doing just that, he pretended that her song choice had gone unnoticed by him as he drove a little way down past Midleton and veered off right just after Loughaderra.

They drove down another narrow road as Roman studied Jasmine, who seemed to be taking in the entire extent of their journey, proving to him that the ditzy party girl routine was only a ruse for the outside world.

Spending time with her the last few days, Roman knew that Jasmine was an intelligent, resilient woman who was not afraid of hard work, who had picked up an axe to chop wood without having to ask her, and when Roman had asked her where she learned to use an axe, the vampire had grinned and simply retorted that she had the blood of Vikings in her veins.

"You're staring at me again, wolf. Stop thinking so hard. You'll only hurt yourself."

"Why do you let everyone think you are this big party girl who is happy to be looked after by her brothers? That's not who you are."

"You don't know anything about me, Roman."

His fingers tightened on the steering wheel. "Like hell I don't. You pretend to be this vapid creature who lives to party all night long, like a trust-fund kid. But I see how you try to make sure everyone is okay. I watched you spar with Isolde before, and you sure as hell don't fight like a woman who has not trained before. You helped Zeke with a contract negotiation when Malakai was in Iceland with Keeva."

"And your point is?"

She didn't even mask the irritation in her tone, as if he had unlocked a huge secret that she had not wanted him to see, like Roman had looked right on through the defences she had erected and she was not thrilled about it. As if, by his knack for assessing people and evaluating their skill set, she had failed in her attempts to shield who she really was from the world.

"Why do you pretend to be something you are not?"

Jasmine stared through the windshield, ignoring his question for an age before she said quietly, a lot softer than he expected from her, "I grew up being treated like glass, but I was a warrior in my blood. When I became a vampire, times had changed. Society changed. Women were expected to be quiet and docile creatures, and so I let someone tell me that who I was, the woman that was opinionated, outspoken, thirsty for knowledge and fun, was the wrong way to be."

Roman felt himself grow angry at whatever asshole had told her that, who had hurt her so badly that she continued to pretend even with him.

"So now I'm Jasmine Cavanagh, party girl," she continued. "She helps me to sneak under the radar. No one expects for the girl dancing on bar tops to go and slit your throat minutes later. It's always the girls like Keeva who you take one look at and know, damn, she could cut a bitch. They never see me coming because I look all sweet and innocent."

Roman barked out a chuckle. "Whoever the fuck takes one look at you and thinks sweet and innocent deserves to have their throat slashed. You know what I first thought when you called me Fido and I was locked into a room with you and Malakai?"

"What?"

Her head was now turned toward Roman as he kept one eye on the road and the other on the blue-eyed vixen next to him.

"I knew with utmost certainty that Malakai could kill me without a second thought, but it was you who drew my attention, it was you that made me think, she could kill me with that smirk on her face and I wouldn't even see it coming. Out of you and Malakai, I considered you the bigger threat."

Jasmine drew back as if surprised by his confession but scenting the truth in his words. Roman steered the car into the car park that suddenly came up on them, right outside the pub that was nestled into absolute nowhere, and stopped the car, shifting so he looked her dead in the eyes as he said, "That asshole who tried to make himself feel good by making you feel less, if he was here in front of me, I would claw him to pieces for you. He didn't deserve to know this side of you. And if I had my way, I would drive us both home so I could take that haunted look off of your face and fuck you so hard that you clawed at my back until you forgot all about him and only of me."

CHAPTER SEVEN

Jasmine

JASMINE BLINKED AT THE RAWNESS OF ROMAN'S WORDS, THE bluntness of them, her body on fire, and she felt her panties dampen. She felt heat in her cheeks, reminding her that it was his blood that enabled her to blush, and that only made her feel even warmer.

She was a vampire, dammit … she wasn't supposed to be getting hot flushes over a werewolf.

And of course, there he was, standing there looking all stern and gorgeous and saying all the right things that were making it very hard to hate him.

Trying to mask her feelings from Roman, Jasmine flicked her hair off her shoulders. "Well as nice as the sentiment sounded, that will never happen. I have made a strict no-shifter policy and don't intend to start now. Guess it's just going to be you and your hand tonight. Soz."

Almost leaping from the car at the sound of Roman's growl, fighting to suppress a shudder, she closed the door and then realized she would have to wait for him before heading into what looked like a very quaint pub that was normally for locals only.

The pub was built like Roman's cabin, giving it a rustic feel that Jasmine found endearing. She knew from looking at it all the decisions that had been carefully made, having put a lot of time and thought into Dante's, whether it was picking out the paint for the walls or what the dance floor would look like. This little place was built with family in mind, built with thoughts of preserving a place for peace and relaxation.

Roman had come to stand beside her, and Jasmine wasn't sure why she suddenly had a spike of anxious energy. She huffed out a breath, sneaking a peek at Roman out of the corner of her eye.

From the very first moment she had met him, Jasmine had felt that pull, that instant attraction and spark from across the room. Roman wasn't like her typical type; then again, her track record with her type wasn't exactly an endorsement for good taste. His well-worn jeans that gave her a very nice view of his ass, with a simple black tee that hugged his toned and muscular body, did nothing to stop Jasmine from wanting to see him naked again soon, despite her declaration to Roman only moments earlier.

"Keep looking at me like that, Jazz, and I may just think you didn't mean what you said."

"Whatever, furball. Are dogs even allowed inside? I can bring you out a little bowl of beer if not," she teased and was surprised at how relieved she was when he chuckled.

"Considering the bar is owned by two werewolves, I think I'm good. First time a vampire's been inside though."

Roman strode forward before Jasmine could splutter a reply, and that made him laugh even louder as he pushed open the door to the bar and held it open for her, Jasmine ducking under his arm to step inside.

Once inside, Jasmine could sense the aura of the place. From the sounds of the soft rock that came from an old-school jukebox and the crackling fireplace to the framed pictures on the walls, this was a place for those within an inner circle. And while the pub was warm and friendly in appearance, the faces in the bar might not be, as several eyes turned to glance in their direction, and Jasmine felt herself reach around for the blades tucked away at her back.

Calloused fingers ensnared her wrist, and she glanced over her shoulder at Roman.

"This is my family, Jazz. You are safe here. With me."

Roman let go of her wrist as a petite curvy woman with brown hair that had faint tinges of red under the lighting set a tray on the countertop and made her way toward them with the biggest and warmest smile on her face. The werewolf beside her stepped forward, and they embraced. A pinprick of irrational jealously put an ache in Jasmine's chest that made her want to snarl at the woman.

The woman reached out and patted Roman on the cheeks as if he were a child. "You look skinnier than the last time we saw you."

"Stop fussing over me, woman."

"Never," the woman said with amusement dancing in her eyes as she turned those hazel-coloured peepers toward Jasmine. "Now introduce me to the absolute stunner standing behind you who looks like she wants to kill me."

Jasmine frowned at the woman's assessment, even as the petite woman grinned and extended her hand. "Abigail Murphy, but everyone calls me Abbie."

Jasmine shook her hand, inhaled, and caught the women's scent, surprised that she had not already scented the fact that Abbie was a werewolf.

"Jasmine Cavanagh. Nice to meet you."

Abbie blinked at the name, glancing at Roman, who was now being greeted by a man who had brown hair and blue eyes that twinkled in the mischievous way that Dylan's always did. The man introduced himself as Conor Murphy, his arms going around Abbie, who rolled her eyes as Conor looked from Roman to her and back again.

"You're defo punching there, mate."

Roman snorted, rolling his eyes in return. "And like you aren't with Abs?"

"But I've got charm and passable looks."

"If you say so, Con. If you say so."

Jasmine watched the exchange with amusement as Abbie linked her arm and dragged her toward a table where more back-slapping and hugging ensued. And more trepidatious glances in her direction.

Jasmine felt the pinpricks of a vision in her mind, but her attention was drawn to the rest of Roman's friends, who kept their eyes on her as Roman pulled out a chair for her beside Abbie. Conor asked Roman what he wanted to drink, then turned to her, a flush on his cheeks as if he didn't know what a vampire would order.

When he eventually did ask, Jasmine gave him one of her biggest smiles, flashing a hint of fang as she said, "I suppose the blood of my enemies isn't on the menu? Shame. Guess I'll settle for whatever cold beer you have on tap."

There was a brief moment of hush where no one uttered a syllable, and then everyone started to laugh, apart from one of Roman's friends who was glaring at her, even as she gave him "just be cool" expressions.

"Everyone, this is Jasmine," Roman started as Jasmine studied the rest of the people at the table, making sure to skim her eyes over them all like she didn't recognise any of them.

"And Jasmine, this is Tyler." Jasmine inclined her head to the man with dark skin and bright eyes.

"And the rest are Réiltín, Hiro, and Ezra."

The other woman was tall, with hair that was streaked at the ends in a variety of colours. Her eyes looked almost black in the darkness, or maybe they were just black. Hiro was a strikingly handsome man with Asian origins, with red hair and green eyes, reminding her a little of Keeva, and when he said hello, she heard the Irishness in his tone.

Ezra's gaze was narrowed. He sneered as he watched Jasmine, who was just about to roll her eyes when she heard

Roman growl. A hint of amber flashed in Ezra's eyes at the implied hostility.

Jasmine had hoped to not bring attention to the fact that she had recognised Ezra and he her, but as she smiled in thanks as Conor handed her a bottle of beer, the air of hostility grew to an almost suffocating level.

"Ezra, spit it out, whatever the fuck you want to say," Conor snapped at the other man, who sank back in his chair with a scowl, or maybe it was a pout.

He looked like a petulant child regardless.

"Just don't like spending my free time with bloodsuckers."

Jasmine heard the pure hatred in his tone and knew it wasn't solely down to the fact she was a vampire, but Jasmine wasn't about to add to the ire by revealing things that Ezra obviously didn't want to be shared, even if he was making it so that there was an atmosphere.

"Still can't believe you take orders from vampires," Ezra spat at Roman, who looked like he was about to reach across the table and smack Ezra's head clean into the table.

Jasmine would have been happy to let it go, but it was part of her job to make sure that discretion was key for employees, especially in the line of work that she and Ezra shared. And Ezra here was making sure that every single member of his team found out how Ezra made his money on the side.

Jasmine took a sip of her beer, then switched to Spanish before she said to Ezra. "Do you want to keep the reason we know each other a secret or not? Keep running your mouth, and Roman will push and push until you tell him."

Ezra's response was to call her a bloodsucking bitch, and Jasmine laughed, surprising the Inferna sitting around the table as she smirked. "Dude, you call me a bitch like it's a bad thing."

That earned a growl from Roman, who had already

looked at him when she said his name. Hiro leaned in and muttered something to Ezra, who glared at him, and Hiro blushed.

Interesting.

Her head began to pulse, the vision that was tapping its way through her defences causing her hand to shake and spill some of her drink.

"Jazz, you okay?"

Everyone was looking at her now, and that made her feel uneasy, because if she went into full seer mode, then the closely guarded secret that they had all kept for centuries would be out in the world, and she didn't know these people well enough to know if she could trust them, even if Roman did.

Before Jasmine could offer up a reassurance that she was fine, Ezra pushed back his chair and stalked to the bar, but not before he cast another withering glance toward her. Hiro offered her an apologetic smile, then went after Ezra. The two men disappeared into a back room.

Conor shook his head, then sat down in the chair beside his mate. "Let me apologize for that dumbass. We hope he hasn't scared you off?"

Jasmine smiled, careful not to show too much fang this time. "It would take more than that to scare me off."

Conor glanced from Jasmine to Roman and back again before he grinned. "Good."

After taking another drink, Jasmine rubbed her head, the pain now a throbbing rather than a dull ache. She waved off Roman's look of concern, turning back to the conversation as the two men came out again. Ezra remained at the bar and Hiro came back, his cheeks flushed as he sank back down on his seat with a huff.

After a few seconds, Jasmine rose, then strode over to where Ezra was sitting. He snarled at her, and all she could do was laugh, ignoring the amber glow in his eyes.

"If you just keep chill, then I won't have to report back to Mac that you almost blew both our covers. I won't spill your secrets, sniper. Don't fucking spill mine."

"I knew this would happen if Roman took a job working for you lot."

"You lot?" Jasmine repeated as she raised a brow. "This lot pays you a lot of money for your skill set. You've had no problems taking our money before, so give it to me straight why it's such a problem now."

When Ezra glanced in Hiro's direction, then realized what he had done, his gaze snapped back to Jasmine with a look that dared her to comment. Instead, Jasmine held up her hands.

"Like seriously? I would have never said a thing. There's a reason we all have code names, dude. It's too hard for assassins to stay in the shadows if we know their names. The only reason I know you is 'cause we met in Tokyo that one time."

Dylan had been lost in one of his depressions, unable to attend the liaison to vet Ezra for the job, so Jasmine had gone instead. They had barely spoken, just shared information about the person who was harvesting Inferna organs and selling them on the Inferna black market.

They had chosen Ezra, as he was a crack shot and never missed a target.

"So if you are worried I'll spill the details, I won't."

"I don't want them to know I get paid to kill people. It's not how we work."

Jasmine rolled her eyes. "To be fair, it's very bad people, but it's grand. Just play polite, and in a few hours, you and me never have to see each other again."

Ezra opened his mouth to retort, halted by Conor, who waved them over, grinning from ear to ear as Jasmine walked back over and settled into her seat.

"Well, since we have a guest tonight, I wanna test her to see if she has what it takes for her to be with our Roman."

"We are not together," both Jasmine and Roman said in unison, earning a titter of laughter from the Inferna seated at the table.

"Enough about that." Conor dismissed their protests. "Jasmine, we want to know if you can pick out what kind of Inferna we all are."

Jasmine wasn't one to back down from a challenge. She ignored the pain building behind her eyes and opened up her senses, closing her eyes to mask the colour change as she let her magic reach out and get a feel for them all. She tasted werewolf and feline shifter, then creatures with mythical auras.

With a smile tugging the corners of her mouth, she opened her eyes again. Pretending to study them all for a few, Jasmine tapped a finger to her chin before she began to speak. "Werewolf," she began, pointing to Roman, who rolled his eyes. Then she pointed to Abbie, Conor, and Ezra. "Werewolves also."

She turned to Tyler, who looked completely positive she would not be able to tell what kind of shifter he was because a normal vampire might not be able to pinpoint his exact species.

But Jasmine Cavanagh was no ordinary vampire.

"Tigris," she said, and Tyler's eyes widened, everyone starting to sit back and pay attention to her now. She glanced at Roman, and his eyes were on hers, his grin wide, and it made her stomach flutter.

Jasmine turned her attention to the remaining two, studying Hiro intently before she inclined her head. "Kitsune."

Hiro sucked in a breath before he asked, "What are you?"

"Can't you tell?" she answered with a coy smile on her face, and that started another round of laughter.

Jasmine focused on the petite woman, staring into her

eyes until Jasmine saw rainbows, much like the woman's hair. "They all know what you are?"

Réiltín nodded. "I have no secrets from them."

Jasmine got to her feet, then strode over to the woman, suddenly a little self-conscious that everyone was looking at her. Jasmine tapped her nose, making a show even though she already knew what Réiltín was, but she wasn't about to say that her visions told her.

"May I?"

The woman giggled. "Sure."

Jasmine crouched down a little, leaned in so that her nose grazed the side of her neck, and inhaled, causing Réiltín to shiver. Then Jasmine straightened, walking slowly back to her seat, making a show to drink her drink before she said, "Unicorn."

There was a moment of silence before Conor let out a whoop of laughter, telling Roman that Jasmine was welcome anytime to join them. After a few minutes of chitchat, the group splintered off into little groups, and that left Jasmine and Abbie alone. The werewolf got up and went to the window, looking out into the night, and beckoned Jasmine over to her.

They chatted about music and Dante's for a while, then Abbie glanced over her shoulder to where Conor and Roman were locked in an intense conversation.

"I adore Roman with all my heart. It makes me happy to see him with you."

Jasmine snorted, rolling her eyes. "He's my bodyguard. Nothing more. I have a strict no-shifter policy."

"If you say so. But we have been a little family, a pack, for a long time, and you are the first woman he has ever brought to meet us. That means something to him."

Jasmine leaned against the window as Abbie pulled over a chair and sat. "He works for my brother, who told him I was not to leave his side. So that's the only reason he dragged me along. I'm glad. It was nice to meet you ... well, some of you."

Abbie laughed softly as pain stabbed in her mind, and she hissed. She vaguely heard Abbie asking if she was okay as the future unfolded behind her now-shut eyes.

Bullets tore through the window, hitting Abbie directly in the forehead. She heard the pained wails of her mate as Abbie hit the ground. A hellhound burst through the door, and as the unicorn tried to influence it, the hound leapt, latching onto Réiltín's neck, the sickening sound of bone snapping echoing.

More shots rang out, hitting their marks, Inferna who were not armed. Jasmine watched the scene unfold, dread in her stomach as Roman went to his knees, and then as Jasmine turned to peer in the direction of the door, a blue-haired creature stepped out of the shadows and the world went black.

Jasmine had mere seconds to come back from the vision, the pain in her head rescinding as she shouted Roman's name, and he turned to look at her as she kicked the legs of Abbie's chair out from under her. The werewolf flattened to the ground before the first shot punctured the glass.

She spun, whipping out her karambits. She yelled "hellhound," then darted toward the door as it burst inward, wood splintering and flying everywhere.

CHAPTER EIGHT

Jasmine

THE SCENT OF FIRE AND BRIMSTONE WAS THE FIRST THING JASMINE caught as she pushed forward, slicing down into the hound's neck, the beast having little time to yelp as Jasmine crossed the karambits and slashed them outwards across its neck. Blood seeped from the wound as the hellhound tried to cry out in pain, but all that managed to slip out was a gargled yelp.

Jasmine had already let the mutt fall to the ground when she felt the hot sting as she was clipped with a bullet, the lead embedding in her shoulder. Paying no attention to the rest of the Inferna in the room, Jasmine let out a snarl as she ducked another stray bullet from a masked Inferna firing from the doorway.

Another hellhound shot past her, leaping over her, its matted fur and red-rimmed eyes a blur. She heard Roman grunt, then growl in response. The Inferna with the gun pulled the trigger again, holding it at an awkward angle as Jasmine surged forward, spinning to kick the gun from his hand, and then she wasted little time in slicing the karambits across his throat.

The Inferna grasped at his throat before dropping to his knees, and then Jasmine ducked outside. The car park was eerily quiet as Jasmine inhaled to catch a scent of anyone who might still be skulking about. Her eyes clashed with eyes of emerald green and a blank expression as a blue-haired

Inferna whistled, the remaining hellhounds all bolting toward her before they just seemed to vanish into the night.

Jasmine heard a commotion in the bar and raced back inside, hearing people shout for Roman to get out of the way, but Jasmine stood in the doorway, transfixed by the werewolf.

Roman's hands had morphed into claws, his eyes were amber bright in the low light, and his mouth, the one that had once been soft and still firm against her own lips, was now widened with teeth to rival her own fangs. His T-shirt was ripped, his arms had claw marks, and he honestly looked like something she had seen in a horror movie.

Berserker … he reminded her of the fabled berserkers.

The hellhound caught her scent in the air and whirled round, its blood-red stare now focused on her. The hound lowered its front legs, readying to strike, then pounced toward Jasmine, who stood holding out her karambits in front of her. However, the hound didn't even get close.

Roman grabbed the hound around the neck and gave a sharp twist, then dropped the dead hellhound to the floor as he panted with exertion. Glancing around, Jasmine saw Abbie and Conor looking at Roman, then at Jasmine.

"Roman," Conor said his name with a familiarness, like he had seen this side of him before, as Roman moved his big body in front of Jasmine, and she heard him growl deep inside his chest.

Conor chuckled, but Jasmine peeked around him and saw Conor move Abbie behind him.

"Calm down, ya langer. I'm not gonna hurt your girl."

Your girl—Jasmine tried very hard not to dwell on those words or the silly girly emotions that flooded her on hearing those words.

Conor held up his hands in submission even as he took a step toward Roman. "The danger is over. But your girl is bleeding. You can't look after her with claws, fella."

Roman's body shuddered, and when he turned, he was

back to normal, his eyes now a delicious hazel once again as he swept his gaze over her. His lips curled into a snarl at the sight of her bloodstained top. Then he shot an amused glance at the blades still clasped in her grip.

"Where the hell did you get them?"

Jasmine curved her lips into a smile. "Birthday present from Dylan. I totally have a girl crush on Maze."

The wolf looked at her with no recognition in his eyes, and Jasmine took a step back.

"Seriously? *Lucifer*? TV show?"

"Jazz, I don't have a TV. How the hell would I know?"

Rolling her eyes so hard that she feared they might just roll out of her head, Jasmine slashed out with her blade so quick, Roman didn't have a chance to react. She cut a strip from his ruined tee and cleaned the blood from her blades, knowing it would have to do until she could clean them properly.

"If you wanted me to take my clothes off, all you had to do was ask."

The huskiness in his tone made Jasmine's toes curl, but she ignored him, sheathing her blades in the custom holster hidden under her jacket. Striding toward the bemused-looking Conor and Abbie, Jasmine offered them an apologetic smile.

"This is on me. Send me the bill, and I'll cover the repairs."

Conor reached out and squeezed her uninjured shoulder. "No need. They come for one of us, Jasmine, they come for us all. They tried to kill my wife, and you saved her life. That debt doesn't go unpaid."

"How did you know?" Abbie asked, scrutinizing Jasmine and making her feel like she was in an interrogation.

"I heard the gunfire," Jasmine said, hoping to pacify the inquisitive wolf.

Abbie's gaze narrowed as if she had scented the lie, then

Conor nudged his wife, who was now looking at Jasmine with less friendly eyes.

"You got somewhere I can get this thing out?"

Conor nodded at her question and told her the back office had a first aid kit and some spare clothes. Jasmine thanked him and then strode through the bar, only stopping when Ezra spat out, "This is all on you."

Jasmine glared at him. "Didn't I just say that? Or are you too dense to think of more than one thing at a time?"

Ezra snarled and took a big step in her direction, shrugging off Hiro, who tried to get him to back down.

"You and your whole family are nothing more than parasites."

"Really? That's all you got? Come on, fleabag, try again."

Veins pulsed in Ezra's forehead as Jasmine laughed, angering the wolf even more. "Or better not try thinking too hard. You might hurt yourself."

Jasmine saw the punch coming and was ready to react when Roman grabbed Ezra's wrist and gave it a squeeze. Ezra dared a glance at Roman, then averted his gaze, leaving Jasmine in no doubt who the most dominant wolf was.

Leaning in so that she held Ezra's gaze, Jasmine offered him a murderous smile. "Behave, little wolf, or I might have an attack of the dumb blondes and tell every single person in here that you are happy to take the parasites' money and kill for it."

Roman sucked in a breath like he was surprised. However, Jasmine was already moving away from them all, and only when she was in the safety of the back room did she hiss at the sting in her shoulder. She perched herself up on the desk, fishing out one of her karambits, preparing to try and dig the bullet out, slipping out of her leather jacket.

"Jesus Christ, woman, what are you doing?"

Peering up at Roman through hooded lashes, Jasmine snorted. "I would have thought that was obvious. I'm getting the bullet out before the skin heals and I have to cut it open again to get it out like they did with Zeke."

"Wait a second," Roman ordered her, and she sighed like he was inconveniencing her.

She put her karambit away again and watched Roman as he opened a filing cabinet, took out a first aid box and pulled a pair of tweezers from it. He then poured some alcohol solution over them, even as Jasmine reminded him, "You know I'm technically dead, right? I can't get an infection."

"Old habits die hard." That was all he said as he came to stand in front of her, using one of his knees to nudge her legs apart, and before she had a chance to argue, Roman was standing between her legs, leaning down to poke at the wound with the tweezers.

She might be dead, but she still felt the fiery ache as Roman poked at the wound until he grabbed the bullet and slowly pulled it out. Jasmine's stomach rolled, and she reached out to dig her nails into Roman's arm.

Then the ache was gone and Roman was scrutinizing the bullet, then the wolf was slipping it into a plastic bag and into his pocket. "Dylan will want to analyse it."

Jasmine pressed her palm to the wound. "Probably a run-of-the-mill bullet that won't have any distinguishing marks, and if there was, they'd have been filed down to disguise it."

Roman set the tweezers down, then his big palm settled over hers as he pulled away her hand to look at the wound. "That should close up fully once you've fed."

Roman held up his wrist, but Jasmine shook her head, drawing a snarl from Roman.

"No quips about dog blood, Jazz. Not tonight."

Jasmine reached out, wanting to roam her hands over his chest, but instead, she rested her palms on his forearms. "I wasn't going to. I just … it's …" She sighed, then felt her shoulders slump. "I don't know your friends, and I don't want to lose myself in the feed and be vulnerable in a strange place where we've already been attacked."

Roman grunted, stepping back to go and rummage in the filing cabinet again, pulling out a small bag with his name on it. He pulled a black tee out of the bag and handed it to Jasmine. "You should put that on."

Jasmine took the T-shirt as Roman stripped off his own, and Jasmine felt her mouth water. His muscles bunched as he made to pull on another T-shirt, his eyes connecting with hers the moment his eyes were visible again. Roman arched his brows in question, or maybe a challenge.

And Jasmine Cavanagh never backed down from a challenge, even if it was with a dangerous-to-her-health wolf.

Jasmine crossed her arms and yanked her vest over her head, hiding her smile behind the fabric as she heard Roman's sharp intake of breath. She dropped the white vest on the desk, looking down to see her bra had her blood on it as well.

"If you take off the bra, then all bets are off, Jazz."

She offered him a look of innocence, meeting his steely, hungry gaze, then slid her eyes down his body, the evidence of his lust straining against his jeans. Her clit thrummed as if urging her to see if Roman would put his money where his mouth was.

It would be wild, and rough, and everything Jasmine had ever craved in bed, and that was nearly enough to toss aside her golden rule to have one dirty night with Roman and get it out of her system.

Then her memories came back to douse the flames of attraction that made her body sing with desire.

Jasmine twisted them so that she straddled Duke, her hands tracing up his chest, wanting to be the one to set the pace. Duke's bored expression sank her heart as he put his hands on her hips.

"What are you doing, Jasmine?"

"I thought we could try something fun."

Duke shook his head, pushing her off his body and sitting up in the bed, the waves of anger almost palpable. *"You've been spending too much time with the degenerate again."*

"That degenerate is my brother. I can spend time with who I like, Duke. And so what if I have? Sex is supposed to be fun and enjoyable. Not something you schedule into your planner."

Duke dismissed her with a wave of his hand. *"Enjoyable sex for a woman is only for those who get paid to enjoy it."*

As handsome as Duke was, as powerful of a vampire as he was, he was still trapped in antiquated, outdated views on what a woman should be like. The sex was bad, more of a chore than an enjoyable experience, and Jasmine craved more, wanted more.

"When Malakai sees my worth, we will live a life where you will be considered a lady in the Inferna, royalty. Try and start acting like it."

Duke got out of the bed and pulled on his trousers, not even sparing Jasmine a glance before he strode from the room and she heard the shower turn on, then his grunts and groans as he got off, and Jasmine was left feeling cold and undesirable.

"What just ran through that mind of yours?"

Though Roman's tone was teasing, Jasmine all but yanked on the T-shirt, the scent leaving her in no doubt that it belonged to Roman. It swam on her, so she pulled the ends and knotted it so that it fit her and wouldn't impede her if she needed to fight again. Her jacket was next, and she shivered as she settled it and then dared to look at Roman.

The wolf stood blocking the doorway, arms folded across his chest, face expressionless. For a minute, she wondered if Roman would probe her to find out what had suddenly made her less flirty, but he kept his lips pressed firmly together.

"I'm gonna have to check in with Malakai. Tell him what happened so he doesn't storm your cabin looking for us."

Roman inclined his head as Jasmine pulled out her phone, called Malakai, and put the phone on speaker.

"Jasmine."

"Okay, so there was a thing and I was shot but I'm okay and no need for you to snarl and order me home." Jasmine swung her legs, heels hitting the table legs, then added. "Oh, and you're on speaker and the wolf has big ears."

"How bad is it, Roman?"

Right, protective big brother mode was being activated. Gotcha.

"Two gunmen, one who breached the pub we were in, and two hellhounds. I killed one, Jasmine the other. When I pulled off the mask of the Inferna who shot Jasmine, his lips were sewn together. We pried them open, and he had no tongue. Looked like a warlock."

"Were you followed?"

"No, sir." Roman's tone gave no indication that Malakai's question had irked him, yet Jasmine spotted the clench of his jaw and the slight tick. "The safe house I took Jasmine to has motion sensors all around the perimeter, with cameras and magic detectors all around. I can send the link to the feed to Dylan if you want to see for yourself."

"That won't be necessary."

"Well," Jasmine drawled as she interjected. "Now that you two have talked shop, let me give you both another piece of information. Remember when Scarlett said she bumped into someone in the bathroom at Dante's and all she can remember is blue hair? She was the one commanding the hounds."

Malakai made a sound like a sigh. "Dylan has been muttering about some blue-haired woman, but he is not making much sense at the moment. We are keeping him close to Scarlett, as he seems to be the calmest near to her. You should answer his texts."

To be honest, Jasmine had been avoiding him for days, not knowing if a text would be classified as contact. The gods didn't tend to be very clear on their visions. When Jasmine didn't respond, she heard Malakai chuckle, then he spoke to Roman again.

"There are still some hours left before dawn. It's not even midnight yet. Bring Jasmine to Dante's, as we had already closed early and are having a meeting there to discuss information. See you soon."

"What about Dylan?" Jasmine blurted out.

"He is already curled up with Scarlett and Zeke watching movies. He won't be there."

The phone clicked on the other side as Jasmine plucked it up and slipped it into her pocket. She was anxious about seeing everyone after her little stint as sleeping beauty, but things were rapidly developing, and even though she might want to run and hide away in the stillness of Roman's cabin, she knew she couldn't idly stand by.

This shadow figure who wanted vengeance on her family, he knew she was a big part in defeating him or else he wouldn't have tried to hobble Sicarius by putting her out of action.

"I've ruined Hiro's birthday, and I didn't even bother to say happy birthday," she mumbled, surprised when Roman laughed.

"That lot? Considering they have been griping at me for taking the job with Sicarius Security so they see little or no action anymore, this will make Hiro's day. I already spoke to Dylan about hiring them next time you guys need more bodies."

"I can tell you now that my brother would hire them all in a heartbeat. I may need to veto Ezra though."

"Does the power of veto work much for you?" he asked with a devilish smile on his lips.

Jasmine shrugged her shoulders. "Not lately. As you recall, I tried to veto your ass."

"I think you're starting to like my ass, Jazz."

Rolling her eyes, Jasmine folded her arm across her chest,

noting the quick shift of his eyes to her chest before returning to her face with a grin. Jasmine shook her head and strode forward. "Move."

"Make me." Roman's tone could only be described as a purr, even if he was trying to challenge her again.

"We don't have time for whatever the hell you are trying to achieve here, Roman. I'm tired and cranky and hungry and just want to get to Dante's so we can go home before the sun rises."

The words were out of her mouth before she had time to process them as Roman flashed her a smug grin, reaching out to tug a blond curl as he teased her. "Ya, I really think you're starting to like me, Jasmine Cavanagh." Roman stepped out of the way, opened the door for her, and then leaned in to whisper in her ear as Jasmine felt herself get a little dizzy at his nearness.

It's the blood loss … it's the blood loss.

But Roman didn't say a thing, simply nipped at her earlobe, and she shrieked in surprise. Embarrassed by the way her bones seemed to melt, she stormed from the room, flicking her hair off her shoulders and ignoring the daring laughter that followed her as she tried to escape the wolf.

CHAPTER NINE

Roman

JASMINE HAD REMAINED QUIET AS SHE LOOKED OUT THE WINDOW of his car, ignoring his attempts to draw a conversation from her. She had offered a hasty goodbye to his friends and waited in the car as Roman said his goodbyes, shaking his head as Conor told him that he liked Jasmine and it was good to see someone have him running a merry chase as his Abbie did.

With a roll of his eyes, Roman mock punched his friend, kissed Abbie on the cheek, and waved to the other members of his team before heading out to the car to see Jasmine inside it, body stiff and tense, and he didn't like it one bit.

She had her eyes closed, and it reminded him of the last seven months, her body lying in her bed, the eerie quiet that was now only drowned out by the hum of the radio. Roman hadn't told anyone how his chest had felt tight for every single night and day that Jasmine had stayed in her magically induced slumber. That he couldn't sleep thinking of her trapped in her own body.

This defeated Jasmine was not the woman who baited him, who taunted and teased him, who fucking set his soul on fire. He hated seeing her like this, and he wanted her to toss a sarcastic comment at him; hell, he'd even settle for her throwing a punch at him if it meant she wasn't so still.

Roman drove back the way they came, heading toward the Cork City centre and toward Dante's. He had worked the door and inside security long enough over the past year to know that this was where Jasmine's heart lay. She came alive, so to speak, when she was in her little DJ booth or passing out drinks to punters. Her smile was infectious, and for a few hours, it was as if he had gotten the truest glimpse of who the vampire was.

She had this aura that just attracted people, and Roman had seen how much her family had unravelled when she was laid up in bed. It was as if she was the glue that held them together, but Roman was pretty sure she had no clue of that position.

He also knew someone had hurt her, could scent her sudden slip of confidence, how she would go from teasing to looking like she had just been slapped. If he ever found the man or the woman who had put that doubt in Jasmine's eyes, he'd tear them to shreds.

His grip on the steering wheel tightened as a possessiveness pushed at him, fraying at his temper. He had no right to be getting possessive of Jasmine. In a few more days, Jasmine would return home and they would go back to the routine of tossing barbs at one another and pretending that the chemistry between them wasn't palpable.

Dammit—he'd told himself that taking Jasmine to his cabin, the place where he had taken no woman before, meant nothing. But the thought of not waking up to her scent in the cabin bothered him more than he thought it would.

Roman felt a muscle in his jaw tick as Jasmine, who must have sensed his dark thoughts, shifted her gaze to look at him, then, after saying nothing, went back to looking out the window, and she kept avoiding speaking to him until they pulled up at Dante's.

Stopping the car, Roman pulled up the handbrake and turned off the engine unbuckling his seat belt as he shifted to Jasmine, holding up his wrist. Jasmine slowly shifted her gaze to his wrist and then to his face.

"I can grab blood inside."

"You really want to go in there still feeling the effects of the bullet? I know you're nearly healed, but it can't hurt to have an extra something in your arsenal."

Truth be told, Roman couldn't stand the thought of her feeding from someone else. He didn't know if he could stand it. The wolf in him was quite clear that they considered Jasmine his, even if the man told him that someone like Jasmine Cavanagh could never be theirs. She was slowly addicting him to her bite, to her, and deep in his soul, Roman felt this time, there was no battling this addiction.

He felt the anticipation of it build inside him as Jasmine sighed, unbuckled herself, and then her fingers were touching his wrist, and he shuddered. Her eyes flared red as if she liked having this control over him, that as much as she craved blood, she liked that he craved her.

Roman watched as her fangs slipped free from her lips, and his heart was hammering like a jackhammer in his chest as she ran her tongue over the pulse on his wrist. His head hit the headrest as Jasmine gently pressed those fangs of hers to his skin.

The skin broke, and then he felt her swallow, hard, and Roman felt his cock harden as he barked out a curse, wanting to drag Jasmine from his wrist and kiss the hell out of her. His growl of frustration reverberated in the car as Jasmine peered up at him from hooded lashes.

Whatever she saw made her flick her tongue over the wound after extracting her fangs. She licked her lips, her fangs still prominent in her mouth, and Roman felt his control snap.

Hand wound in her hair, he yanked her forward, crashing his lips to hers, eliciting a groan from them both. They kissed, all tongues and teeth and pent-up lust. When Roman licked his tongue along one of her fangs, Jasmine moaned into his mouth, and the sound made his hips rock upward, frustrated that there was nothing feminine to press his hardness against.

Moving with vampire speed, Jasmine was suddenly in his lap, exactly where he wanted her, the steering wheel meaning she had to get even closer to him. Jasmine dragged her nails across his scalp, and Roman rolled his hips again, his hands cupping the underside of her breasts as Jasmine pulled back from the kiss, the red gone from her eyes, her fangs sheathed but the hunger in her eyes was still present.

Roman slowly moved his thumb along the curve of her breasts, giving her space to opt out if it was only the blood haze that made her want to get up close and personal with him. His chest was heaving and he was seconds away from losing the last grip on his control when there came a sharp tap on the window.

Jasmine blew out a frustrated breath as she rolled down the window, and while Roman was thankful it wasn't one of her brothers, having Keeva grin at them through the lowered glass meant he would not hear the last of it.

"If you two are finished making out like teenagers in the car, everyone is waiting on you two before this meeting begins."

Keeva laughed as Jasmine just put back up the window and righted her clothes. She opened the door, looking at him, when Roman grumbled that he needed a minute.

Jasmine dipped her gaze to his crotch, then it darted back up, her expression blank for a second before she offered him a very deliberate smile. "Down, boy."

Roman growled as she slipped out of the car and shouted after her. "Not fucking funny, Jazz."

The minx just laughed harder as she shut the door and Roman tried to readjust himself. He pulled his tee out of the waistband of his jeans, letting it hang loose, and then he got out of the car, spotting Keeva leaning against the wall and Jasmine standing in front of her. The two women were chatting as Roman drew closer. Jasmine glanced at him, and then her eyes went that milky shade of white.

"Rivers of blood flow through the streets. Vengeance can be his. The heart of the prince can be lost in a war of hearts. The wolf is howling at our door, and he will huff and puff until we all fall down. The babe is the first to fall; death is the catalyst. One by one, all the king's horses and all the king's men all fall down."

Jasmine cackled—that was the only way Roman could describe it—as Malakai stepped out the side door, holding up a hand to Roman when he would have reached for Jasmine.

"Best to leave her be when she is caught up in the future."

Roman trusted the other vampire to know what was best for his sister as she spun around and looked at Malakai, who merely arched his brow, betraying no emotion.

"The wolf is howling at your door. Arrrooo!" Jasmine gave an impressive howl into the night before she continued. "They are not safe in the tower; they are not safe from him. I can see him now, bathed in shadows. The eye of Horus protects him. The wolf is howling at our door, and he will huff and puff until we all fall down. The war of hearts has just begun."

Jasmine blinked as the milkiness drained from her eyes, leaving frustration and anger. "For fuck sake!" She stomped a foot in temper and lifted her eyes to the sky. "You obviously want me to stop this, so how about you give me something we can work with?"

The sky did not answer her, and Jasmine shook her head.

Malakai stepped forward with a soft smile. "You're okay? No aftereffects after being shot?"

"Nope. Roman cleaned the wound and I had blood. I'm good to go."

"Oh thank god," said Keeva, leaning into Malakai's shoulder, the gesture making Roman's chest ache. "If I have to answer one more stupid question from male vampires who cannot understand that I'm an assassin by trade, Imma start touching some dickheads. The urge to kill is overwhelming in my fragile female state."

That made Malakai chuckle, even as Jasmine rolled her eyes. "Welcome to the world of male vampires, who seem stuck back in the dark ages. There are so many of them that they think themselves superior. Present company excluded, Kai."

"I'm touched," Malakai drawled, then he continued to study Jazz as he said, "Jazz, you should know Thorpe is here. He came in with Radu this evening from a scouting mission in Romania."

If Jasmine could have paled, Roman knew she would have, as her entire body tensed, then she flicked her hair off her shoulders. "It's all good. I had to bump into him eventually. I mean, I managed to avoid him for fifty years."

"You should know that you also smell like Roman, so I assume that's his T-shirt you're wearing."

"Yup. Bored now. Can we go?"

Jasmine sauntered off without waiting for an answer. Malakai dropping a kiss to Keeva's cheek before he followed after her. Roman couldn't stop his eyes from wandering down to watch Jasmine's curvy ass as she walked.

"Dude, eyes off the boss's ass."

Roman bumped shoulders with the flamed-haired assassin. "You gonna lie to me and tell me that you weren't checking out Malakai?"

Keeva snorted, shrugging her shoulders. "'Course I was. But I'm marrying him. I get to check out the goods." She glanced up at him as they walked toward the back entrance. "I should tell you to remember that this is a job and you don't get paid to mess around with Jazz, but I fell for Malakai while trying to kill him. Hell, even Scarlett managed to tame the untameable while she was supposed to be working. I must get someone to test the water in Sicarius to see if there is something in the water."

Roman laughed out loud. Jasmine cast a glance over her shoulder at him, frowned, then snapped her head back around. They would finish what they started in the car, Roman was determined, but for now, it was all about keeping the family and that unborn baby safe.

Jasmine had stopped just inside the main floor of Dante's as Malakai leaned in and said something he didn't quite catch. Malakai moved forward, toward the group of four vampires and Isolde, as Keeva strutted forward to where Isolde was standing.

"Okay, next guess. Phoenix?"

The other woman shifted her eyes to Keeva for a moment, then with a slightly annoyed expression on her face, she continued to ignore Keeva as she continued to try and figure out what kind of Inferna Isolde was. Keeva had been trying to figure it out since she first came to Sicarius, but his friend was having no luck at all.

And watching Isolde growing ever more impatient was actually hilarious.

Roman stood next to Jasmine, her body rigid as she scanned the room, eyes falling on the group Malakai was talking to. He angled his body slightly, motioned for them to join the group as Jasmine muttered, "Let's get this over with."

With a fake-ass smile plastered on her lips, Jasmine strode over, and he followed after her, his own eyes scanning the vampires who had now turned their attention to Jasmine.

"Gents," Malakai began, waiting until Keeva and Isolde had also joined them before he continued. "For those of you who have not met him before, this is Roman Lowe. He was recently promoted to second-in-command of security alongside Isolde by Dylan."

Most of the vampires inclined their heads, but one just stared at him like his presence was a particular inconvenience to him. Roman let his eyes skip over the vampire, yet he needed to take stock of these vampires, for they would not be within Malakai's circle unless they were dangerous.

"Roman, let me introduce Radu Dragomir, prince of Romania."

Radu was exactly what you expected a vampire to look like, the Hollywood stereotypical pale skin, eyes so dark they were almost black, with long black hair that hung loose down to his waist. He wore a black ensemble, down to the cloak that swept the floor when he moved. The vampire felt old. It seemed to leak from his pores as Radu bowed his head, but he didn't say anything as Malakai moved on.

"This is Nadeem." Malakai offered no explanation for the vampire with warm sun-kissed skin. Roman had worked enough in foreign countries to guess that Nadeem hailed from somewhere in eastern regions, but when the man spoke, he held no hint of an accent.

"It is a pleasure to meet you. Dylan, he speaks highly of you." Nadeem smiled, running a hand through his curly brown hair, then grinned at Jasmine. "Lady Jasmine. Have you decided to ditch the bleakness of Ireland and the cold and come and become a princess of sand and sun?"

Roman bristled, easing when Jasmine offered him a warm laugh. "And join that harem of women who even now mourn that you aren't in bed with them? I think not."

"A man can but dream."

"And now that Nadeem has stopped flirting with my sister, this is Jurgen."

The vampire was pale also, with white-blond hair and blue eyes. He grunted a response, and Malakai said something to him in German, but the vampire didn't give Roman a second glance as he frowned and kept silent.

"You'll have to excuse Jurgen," Jasmine began, her tone even and clipped as if she didn't like the fact that the vampire looked at Roman like he was something on the bottom of his shoe. "The packs in Germany hunt vampires for sport. He dislikes shifters."

"As I recall, Jasmine, you also had a dislike for shifters, especially werewolves. Have you managed to disregard your distaste in the time since I had laid eyes on you?"

Roman paid close attention to the other vampire who was looking at Jasmine with disapproval in his eyes and his tone. Both man and wolf immediately disliked the vampire, even before he felt Jasmine bristle by his side.

"A lot can change in fifty years."

There was a coldness in Jasmine's tone that Roman had never heard before, as if it cost her a little to even speak to the vampire who was smugly looking at them, and it made Roman want to punch him.

His accent was definitely aristocratic, yet to Roman, who had a decent ear for accents, felt like it was an accent that the vampire had taken on rather than the one he was born with. His skin was a rich hazel, not as dark as Nadeem's but more of the tone of someone born to biracial parents. He wore navy slacks, a white shirt, and some sort of jacket that reminded him of an outfit he had seen in one of those *Pride and Prejudice* films Abbie had made them watch during one deployment.

The vampire's eyes were golden, his hair shaven short, and he just looked clean, polished. He was looking at Jasmine with a familiarity that irked Roman, even as the vampire stepped forward and reached for Jasmine's hand, who snatched it away before he could touch her.

Roman growled.

With a click of his tongue, the vampire made to reach for Jasmine again, and Roman took a step closer.

"Really, Jasmine. Call off the guard dog. Can we not have a civil greeting with one another?"

Jasmine reached out and squeezed Roman's elbow, and the dickhead watched the interaction, even though Jasmine said nothing to Roman, addressing the vampire instead.

"If you keep calling him a dog, Duke, I might just see if his bark is worse than his bite."

The asshole tried again to reach for Jasmine, but Roman snapped out his hand and grabbed the vampire by the wrist. "Try and touch her again without her permission, and I will break it."

"Thorpe, that's enough." Malakai chastised the other vampire yet said nothing to Roman, who let go of his wrist and stepped back even as the vampire glared at him.

"I think you two know each other well enough now, but Roman, this is Colin Thorpe."

The vampire, who obviously had a death wish, extended his hand to Roman. "Those who know better call me Duke, as is befitting of my station. You shall call me it thus."

"Why?"

CHAPTER TEN

Jasmine

"I BEG YOUR PARDON?"

Jasmine barely held back a chortle of laughter at the sight of Duke's face as Roman kept a cool and calm expression. Malakai had to bite back a smile, even as his banshee was grinning like an idiot.

"You heard me," Roman replied to Duke, folding his arms across his broad chest. "Why should I call you Duke? Malakai introduced Radu as a prince, so I would expect to call him something befitting his title. I was introduced to you as Colin Thorpe. Why should I call you Duke?"

Duke looked at Malakai, who simply shrugged. "The man asked you a question. Only you can answer it."

For a delicious moment, Duke looked like he had absolutely no clue what to do, but then he began to speak. "My father was a duke. Had I not been reborn as a vampire, I would have claimed the title upon his death. As his only son, when he died, even though publicly, it could not be bestowed upon me as my rightful claim."

"So not a duke at all. Stupid to give yourself a nickname when it doesn't apply to you."

"You will call me Duke as is my right!"

Oh my god, Duke was losing his mind at Roman right now, and Jasmine wasn't ashamed to say she was thoroughly enjoying the interaction. She heard the way Duke's voice shrilled as he tried to order Roman about like the wolf would listen to him.

"Let me get this straight. Your father, the duke, had a fumble with one of the staff, and you were born. He had no other sons with his wife, and that makes you think you have a claim to the title? Nah, I think I'll call you Colin. Always thought it was a perfect name for an asshole. I've met a lot of stupid people in my life, Colin, but you could be the stupidest."

"How dare you!" Duke exclaimed and took a dangerous step toward Roman.

Jasmine had seen Roman fight, knew he sparred with Keeva, Malakai, Dylan, and even Zeke numerous times, and if she had to put money on who would win in a fight, her money would be on Roman.

Just when the evening was about to get interesting, Malakai said, "Roman, stand down."

Jasmine watched as the wolf inclined his head respectfully at Malakai, then just said, "Yes, sir."

In the space of five minutes, Roman had calmly put Duke back in his place and shown the other vampires how much respect he had for Malakai by obeying his request, falling into a resting stance.

Colin fumed, looking like he was going to argue, then glanced at Malakai before he sighed and remarked to her, "We can speak after."

"I'd rather not."

Malakai interjected again, asking everyone to sit down, Duke visibly seething when Jasmine took the seat next to Malakai and Roman stood behind her. Isolde had placed herself between him and Keeva, who declined a chair when Malakai offered one to her and stood with the rest of the guards.

"Nadeem, tell me what you discovered," Malakai asked as he leaned back in his chair as if he wanted to get closer to the banshee at his back.

"Perhaps we should wait until the women depart. This is not the type of conversation that they should be privy to."

Jasmine was already shaking her head as Malakai leaned forward. "If their presence disturbs you, Thorpe, then perhaps you should leave. Jasmine holds a higher place in my Kiss than you do, and she is far more useful than you have ever been. Isolde could end you without breaking a sweat, and Keeva, well, you won't see her coming. She earned the nickname Death because she is literally death in Inferna skin. If you want to test any of them, I'm sure we would all like to see you put on your ass."

"The lack of respect in this room does not make me feel welcome."

"Malakai only asked you to come so that we had someone to shield us should someone start firing golden bullets, Thorpe." Nadeem chuckled as the other vampire glared at him, and she could have kissed Nadeem for it.

"Then let them fetch us refreshments and make themselves useful."

Jasmine made to answer, but it was Keeva who got there before her. "If you want me to put poison in your drink, sure, Colin, I'll get you a drink."

When Duke cast her a glance and then dismissed her without answering, Keeva's cheeks flushed with anger. "Hello? You hard of hearing over there? I'm talking to you."

"I will not lower myself to answer a ruffian like you."

Jasmine felt Malakai bristle, even as Keeva laughed, a harsh sound, before she retorted, "Is your dick really that small that you have to put down anyone who you think less of? I knew a douchebag like you before … just like you, he underestimated me, treated me like a dog on a leash, but you know what happens when you keep poking at someone? They bite back. And I didn't even flinch as I put a bullet in his head. It's been a while since I used my powers. Maybe I need to flex myself to see if I still have it."

Duke still continued to ignore Keeva. "Do you let her speak to you like so?"

Then it was her brother's turn to chuckle. "I consider it foreplay when she gets angry at me. She tends to break quite a few phones around me. I fell for a warrior, Thorpe. I did not fall for a docile fawn who cannot hold her own. But keep looking at her with disdain, and I will sit back and enjoy it as she makes you kneel before her like the queen she is."

Keeva grinned a feral smile as Duke clucked his tongue again.

"Men like you should have stayed in the dark ages, Colin. The Inferna world is not purely a male dick-measuring contest. Perhaps you should just jog off back to merry ole England and leave the grown-ups to get on with things."

Duke didn't respond to Keeva, but Malakai reached up and patted her arm. Nadeem was grinning from ear to ear, apparently highly amused at how Duke kept getting put down.

"As amusing as all this is, let me tell you what I found," Nadeem remarked as he got to his feet, strode to the bar and, leaning over the counter, snagged a bottle of beer. "This Vindicta has been stretching out his grasp to the far regions of the world, looking to gather as much information about you lot as possible, and anyone who gives the information winds up dead."

"He must not like leaving loose ends alive," Radu interjected, the rest of the group nodding in agreement.

"I have heard rumours, whispers on the wind that he had been searching for ancient scrolls. Ones that predate the Inferna. I spoke with a Jinn who told me that he was asked by a blue-haired minion of this Vindicta how to bind blood to an object."

Pain pierced her head for a second, and then Jasmine

closed her eyes, trapped in a vision so suddenly that she had little time to shield herself. She felt Roman's knuckles graze her neck, and she let the vision take hold.

She stood on Parnell Bridge, soot and ash on her skin, the scent of blood in the air. The ground rumbled beneath her feet. She heard screams and cries as winged beasts flew overhead. She had been in this vision now, yet it felt more like she was walking in someone's dream rather than glimpsing a snippet of the future.

"You alone cannot stop me."

Jasmine whirled around and whipped out her karambits. The shadowy figure was just a blur in the apocalyptic setting. She heard a soft fussing noise and realized that this Vindicta was holding Grayce in his arms. Yet it was not a mere baby that he held but a toddler, one that had Scarlett's dark tresses and piercing blue eyes. The toddler had Zeke's strong jaw and nose, and she lifted her hand to wave at Jasmine like she knew her.

"You will not harm the child."

"Death tried to stop me, and she has fallen. The obscurum tried, and his ashes now coat your skin, unable to save his child. Her blood will open the door. And then the world will be anew."

The dead body of Malakai's soul mate lay at the monster's feet, her lifeless eyes having lost that fire those green eyes of hers always held. The blurry figure shimmered, a pulse of magic, before he lifted a gun and pulled the trigger, and Jasmine was yanked from the vision.

Jasmine clutched at her chest as if she could feel the bullet rip through her. She gulped in a breath, not that she needed it, but panic flooded through her as she tried to recall every minute detail of the vision.

Strong hands cupped her face, pulling her eyes to rich, warm, hazel ones.

"Hey, Jazz. Just look at me. Ride it out and look at me."

There was a slight order in his tone, but it helped her focus. Roman was crouched in front of her, his big body blocking out the rest of the group as Roman winked at her. "Tell us what you saw, darling."

"Vindicta is trying to open a door, to what I'm not sure. He wants to use the baby's blood to open it. He wants to remake the world anew, whatever that means. I could see everything clearly but him." Dragging her gaze from Roman's, she looked over at Malakai. "He's using magic, powerful magic to shield himself. That's why I can't see him."

"Anything else?"

Swallowing hard, Jasmine reached out and placed her hands on Roman's chest, and he took his hands away from her face. "If he succeeds, Keeva and Zeke will die trying to rescue her."

Keeva whistled between her teeth. "Then we just need to make sure that we catch the fucker before he gets to kill me. No biggie."

Malakai rose from his seat, buttoning up his suit jacket, but Jasmine saw her brother's fingers tremble. "Nadeem, try and get as much information as possible. Use every favour I have ever acquired if you need it."

"If word of this—what was the phrase your lovely bride used before?—*douchebag* is spoken and the winds hear it, then I will let you know. I have known you a long time, Malakai. My blade is yours."

Jasmine grinned at the vampire as she waited for Roman to rise, then Nadeem reached for her hand. She was aware Duke watched her, so she let Nadeem press his lips to the back of her hand with a cheeky grin, and then the vampire who heard secrets on the wind headed for the door after a quick word to Keeva.

Radu seemed to vanish into the shadows, silent as ever, but he was loyal to Malakai. Duke stayed where he was, his eyes on her as she felt herself shrink back, knowing that exact look, one that usually came before he berated her in private.

"Why are you dressed like a whore?"

"Do you want men to think you are easy?"

"You should leave the thoughts to the men, Jasmine. It is not becoming for a lady to think as much."

"Were it not for the fact that you are striking, that being with you did not increase my station, I would not bother to share my bed with you. That mouth of yours is more trouble than it's worth."

Duke had never been violent toward her, yet it took Jasmine a while to realize that there were different kinds of abuse, and his words, his actions, had crippled her confidence and made her feel worthless. She hadn't even realized it herself; such was the nature of his control. It had taken a mental breakdown from Dylan, who had sucked all of her emotions from her, resulting in Malakai sending Duke away.

And when Duke had asked her to go with him, Jasmine had found it in herself to say no.

She had clawed back the person she had been before Duke, had changed because of it, and she would not go back to feeling that way anymore.

"I would take my leave. Jasmine, a word?"

Jasmine stood her ground, made him come to her, and Roman stayed by her side, a silent but comforting presence. Duke seemed annoyed that Jasmine didn't ask Roman to leave, looked like he was about to, then changed his mind.

"I must leave tomorrow, but I wanted to take you to dinner before I go. We have a lot to discuss. In private."

Jasmine looked at Duke, really looked at him. Sure, he was handsome - he had those chiselled good looks you would expect from a leading man in the movies. When he had first smiled at her after Malakai had introduced them, his eyes had brightened, and she had nearly swooned, but it had all been an act. She had been attracted to him, and Malakai had seemed to like him, so she had agreed to a date.

Now, Jasmine could honestly say that any attraction had been eliminated completely. She considered how she had to force her body to react as Duke wanted, to arch her body like she was supposed to do, to pant and moan even when his touch did nothing for her.

Instead, she had kissed Roman only a handful of times, and her body had felt like it was aflame. That was how attraction should be between two people. Not a cold transaction that left her feeling empty afterwards.

Jasmine snorted. "We have nothing to discuss. Our time together is something I try not to dwell on. You're just lucky I didn't respond when Keeva asked if your dick was really that small."

"Have I not told you before how much I find your foul mouth distasteful."

"You poor bastard," Roman laughed as he gave Duke a feral smile. "You had her, and you threw her away. I've tasted those lips, mate, and there's nothing distasteful about 'em. Jasmine has been trading smart remarks for me for almost a year, and every single time she does, I want to capture that mouth of hers with my own and taste her. I feel sorry for ya, mate. You couldn't appreciate the gift you had."

Roman reached for the lapels of Duke's shirt and yanked him forward a little. "Jasmine has made it perfectly clear that she wants nothing to do with you. Can't say I'm surprised. But I'm telling you that should you ever dare speak to her like she is dirt, I will use claws and teeth to rip you to shreds."

Roman let go of Duke, and he stumbled back, a look of pure astonishment on his face. He smoothed down his clothing as if he wanted to brush away Roman's hands as he glanced at Jasmine, then back to Roman.

"It's like fucking a cold fish, wolf. Just remember that."

"She certainly didn't feel like a cold fish when she was straddling my waist in the car 'bout half an hour ago. Maybe all she needs is a man who knows what to do with his hands, mouth, and his …"

Jasmine elbowed Roman hard in the ribs to stop him from finishing that sentence, but the wolf just grinned. Duke huffed and puffed out his chest, but Jasmine held up her hand.

"Don't. Whatever comes out of your mouth next, no matter what it is, and I let him off the leash. If you don't want your fangs knocked into your stomach by him or me, get out of my club, *Colin.*"

The other vampire hissed as she called him by his given name, then turned on his heels and was gone in the blink of an eye. Jasmine might have sagged in relief if she was not pissed as hell at Roman for talking so that everyone in the room knew they'd been fooling around.

She was about to whirl on Roman when Keeva came up to them, laughing. "That was awesome. I half wanted someone to kick him in the nuts, but after that comment, Jazz, I'm not sure you'd hit anything."

"I've gotten off harder by myself than I ever did with him," Jasmine remarked, a flare of heat flared in Roman's gaze before Malakai called him over.

"Still haven't gotten down and dirty then?"

"Not happening," Jasmine grumbled as Keeva laughed again.

"You two were seconds away from doing something in the car that might get you arrested. At least find an office with a locked door." Keeva grinned, muttering about only having a few days left before normality struck.

Jasmine lifted her gaze to see Roman staring right at her, his intentions clear in his eyes even as he nodded at something Malakai said, but Jasmine wasn't listening to anything. Her entire body felt alive and resolute as she made a decision.

She was done fighting destiny. She was done fighting what she wanted.

A vision punched into her mind, of Roman with his mouth on her core, her head thrown back, her spine arched as she fisted her hands in the sheets. Roman's tongue plunged in and out of her, and Jasmine felt herself shudder, and then

Roman was striding toward her, hunger in his eyes, as if he had seen what she had and he wanted a bite out of her.

She might just let him. She might actually want him to bite her, just like he had nipped at her earlobe, but in other places. Jasmine waved over her shoulder, ignoring Keeva's grin and Malakai's obvious discomfort as Roman placed a hand on the small of her back, the touch almost searing through her, leading her out into the night air and toward the car.

CHAPTER ELEVEN

Roman

ROMAN COULD FEEL JASMINE WATCHING HIM, FELT THE WEIGHT of her gaze on him, and even caught sight of a slightly amused smile tugging at the corners of her lips. He was close to snapping, to losing his control. He needed to run it off. This happened to him whenever he pushed down the instincts of the wolf, which was to rip Colin fucking Thorpe to shreds for hurting Jasmine.

"If you grip the steering wheel any harder, you'll break it." Jasmine held up her hands as he slid his eyes toward her. "Hey, just saying. If you wanna talk about whatever's going on in your head, then pull over and we can talk."

"We can talk when we get back home." The words tumbled from his lips before he could process what he was saying, but the little quirk of Jasmine's lips gave him hope this could be something.

"Sure, okay … but ease up on the wheel, or it will take even longer."

Roman swallowed hard. However, he did as Jasmine asked and eased his grip on the steering wheel. He was still trying to process what Malakai had whispered in his mind, not having known that the head vampire had any powers like his sister and brother.

"He fooled us all, and we did not see it until he had nearly broken her spirit. Dylan tried, and it pushed her further toward

him. I'd kill him for it, yet we would be the first suspects in his murder."

"Why are you telling me this?" Roman pushed the thought into his head.

"Because I can see it in your eyes, hers too, how much attraction there is there. And if you hurt her, I'll be the one to come for you."

Roman had already planned to act on his feelings, to seduce and tease Jasmine like she deserved before he worshipped her body. He wanted to taste every inch of her, feast himself on her taste. Would she taste like honey when he lapped at her wetness? A low growl rumbled in his chest, and Jasmine arched her brow.

"What thought in your head made you go all snarly?"

Roman barked out a laugh. "You don't want to know."

"Try me."

Roman steered the car toward his cabin, taking a few minutes to gather his thoughts before he said quietly, a roughness in his tone, "I was wondering if you would taste like honey when I dragged my tongue along your wet core. Would you be tight when I dipped in a finger? I wanted to know how much it would take before I could make you purr and make sure you screamed my name. If I touched you now, would you already be wet and ready for my tongue?"

Jasmine's mouth hung open like she was having trouble finding the words to respond to him, and that made Roman chuckle. She snapped her mouth shut, then that devious smile of hers lit up her face. She slipped her hand inside the waistband of her pants and let out a moan that made his cock twitch.

Jasmine removed her hand, her fingers glistening as she said, "Definitely wet."

Roman growled, snatching her hand and thrusting those two fingers into his mouth and sucking hard, his own groan reverberating around the car as Jasmine shivered. His blood thrummed with anticipation, the thought that finally after months of stroking himself to thoughts of this vampire, he was going to have her.

A moment of self-consciousness flashed in her eyes as Roman gave her fingers one more suck and then released them. The car ground to a stop, and Jasmine bolted from the car. The wolf howled, wanting to chase its mate, but Roman shook it off because if he chased her, he would strip and mount her in the forest, and he wanted to savour this first time with her.

"Jasmine." He said her name, and the pain in his voice must have made her stop because she turned to look at him. "Don't run. If you run, the wolf will push me to chase you. Please. I'm on a knife-edge here."

"Okay." That was all she said before walking, slowly, into the cabin.

Roman followed after her, closing the door behind him as Jasmine started making coffee. She had kicked off her heels and jacket, and Roman slipped off his shirt and shoes too, sitting down on the couch as he left Jasmine to make the coffee. He felt a swell in his chest as she handed him a coffee and then sat next to him on the couch, folding her legs under her so she faced him. Roman shifted so that his arm rested on the back of the couch.

"I bet you're thinking I'm a fool." It was a statement rather than a question.

"I told you what I was thinking in the car. The word fool never came to mind."

Jasmine rolled her eyes and sipped her coffee as a flush of heat rose on her cheeks. "He was the perfect boyfriend to begin with. Flowers, gifts, dinners; he treated me like a princess, and I loved it. I liked him, but I was never attracted to him, I guess."

"But you wanted to give it time to see if your feelings changed."

"Exactly." She replied with a smile. "But then he started to want to change me. Didn't like me hanging with Dylan, said he was a bad influence. Didn't like the idea of us opening Dante's, so I never told him about the side gig. When we went out, he picked out my clothes, told me what to eat and drink and how to act. If I didn't do what he wanted me to, he would scream at me for making him look like a fool who could not control his woman."

"I should have clawed the bastard to death."

Sipping her coffee again, Jasmine snorted. "I should have done that myself. I could have."

"I saw how you took out the hellhound. I'd watch you fight anytime."

Brightness swarmed her eyes. "You know, for a wolf, you always seem to say the right things."

"I find telling the truth helps with that."

She dismissed him with a wave of her fingers. "Anyways. Dylan and I had fallen out because my brother tried to tell me what was happening, and I believed Colin's words, that Dylan was a bad influence, that his sexual tastes were not becoming for a vampire of his station. That Malakai really need a number two with better values who could help elevate the Kiss. I thought he had meant me, but he was using me to get closer to Malakai."

Jasmine's eyes dropped to her coffee, and Roman reached out and tugged a strand of hair. "I suppose you want to know why he said I was a cold fish in bed."

"You don't have to tell me anything you don't want me to know."

She peered up at him, big blue eyes that reminded him of the clearest ocean waters, as if she expected him to demand she tell him all the sordid details. Then she bobbed her head before she began speaking again.

"I had a few lovers before him, nothing exciting that made me agree with Dylan about how mind-blowing sex was. I thought maybe it was men that didn't excite me, so I tried with women, and every experience just left me feeling cold. With Colin, it was very vanilla."

"Vanilla?"

Jasmine laughed then, a soft sound. "Dylan calls normal sex vanilla. He describes his nights out in terms of ice cream flavours. Vanilla was me lying on the bed while Colin lasted about three minutes. I faked … I mean, he didn't like kissing during sex or dirty talk or anything that he considered kinky."

Roman was stunned. Shocked beyond all belief. That absolute bell-end had this gorgeous, smart, feisty female naked in bed with him, and he couldn't even fuck her right. Just as he was about to tell her that, another thought popped into his head.

"Jazz, did he at least get you off some?"

She squirmed in her seat, shaking her head. "Hell, this is embarrassing. I feel utterly fucking embarrassed telling you all this." Jasmine set down her coffee. "He would check to see if I was wet, and if not, he would use lube. It was always my fault I wasn't ready for him. Not that it mattered. He wasn't exactly well hung."

Roman barked out a laugh, letting the wolf into his eyes as he studied his prey. He understood her now, the teasing and then the immediate retreat. She had been told her sexuality was unbecoming, that her wants and needs were secondary to her partner's.

Not with him. Never with him.

"And what fantasies does Jasmine Cavanagh have hidden in that super-smart mind of hers?"

Jasmine jerked up off the couch and stalked to the window, gazing out into the weaning night. The moonlight kissed her skin, bathing her in the faint tinge of its beam, and she looked breathtaking.

Roman set his mug down on the table and decided to

change tactics. "You said your previous experiences left you feeling cold. What do you feel when I touch you?"

"Like my entire body is on fire. Like I'm alive again."

That made Roman grin with smugness as he stalked toward Jasmine. "And have you been thinking about what you would like to do about that?"

He tried to keep his tone even, calm, coaxing, yet it was hard to mask the huskiness in his tone as Jasmine pressed her back against the wall of the cabin. "If I said yes?"

Roman stopped just outside of touching distance. "Tell me." There was a little push of an order, even as her eyes widened, and when it looked like Jasmine might bolt, he gave her a wolfish smile. "Talk dirty to me, Jasmine Cavanagh."

Jasmine flicked her tongue over her lips, and he followed the movement, wanting to close the distance between them and lose himself in a searing kiss that would undo them both.

"I want to touch you, skin to skin. I want to hear your heart racing as I touch and taste you. I want …" She hesitated, then it was like Jasmine just threw caution to the wind. "I want to dig my nails into your skin and see if you growl like you did when I dragged them on your scalp. I want to take your cock in my hands, then my mouth before I straddle you."

Roman was on board for all of the above and then some. He stayed rooted to the spot, letting Jasmine come toward him, her hands tracing up his arms, and he shuddered, her touch as addictive as her bite.

"I want to sink my fangs into you when you are inside me."

Roman couldn't stop the involuntary jerk of his hips, and that caused Jasmine to laugh, a throaty sound that made his cock feel like a steel rod. Jasmine had begun to feel along his chest as she said quietly, "But most of all … I had a vision … of you and me, and I want to know if it's real. I ache to know if it's real."

"What did you see?" he managed to ask, his skin tight, and the need to clamp his teeth down and mark her made him shudder again.

"Let me show you."

Roman blinked as Jasmine touched his forehead with her fingers, and then he saw himself on his knees, his mouth latched on to Jasmine's core, and he tasted her on his tongue as if he was the one making her back bow and her fingers grip the sheets.

The vision vanished, and the chains on Roman's control snapped. His mouth crashed down on hers, his hands in her hair, and she kissed him back with as much eagerness and pent-up lust that their teeth bashed, their noses bumped, but he was kissing Jasmine and she was kissing him and he only pulled away when he needed to catch his breath, his chest heaving.

Roman pressed a kiss to her lips, his hand stroking down her sides, and then he boldly cupped her ass and lifted her. Jasmine immediately wrapped her legs around his waist, linking her arms around his neck. He walked forward, Jasmine nipping the curve of his jaw, and then he tossed her on the bed, his vampire letting out a peal of laughter as she bounced .

He pulled his tee over his head as Jasmine licked her lips and made him feel like a king. She made to strip off her own top, but Roman shook his head.

"I've been wanting to unwrap you since the night you put ideas of leashes and collars into my mind. We can save that for later."

They kissed again, breaking apart so Roman could remove the tee he had loaned her, then his lips were on her skin, her hands were in his hair as he trailed his lips down her jaw, her neck, the swell of her breasts. Her eyes were wide, yet he saw no confusion or lack of self-confidence as she reached down and unclasped the front of the bra, her mouth-watering breasts spilling out as she tossed the bra aside.

"I dreamed about having my hands on those perfect handfuls. I fantasised about using my teeth on those pert nipples while I fisted my cock in the shower." He heard Jasmine growl and looked up to see tinges of red in her eyes. "Do you like to hear that I could only come thinking of your hands, your mouth on me? That I crave you. That I've had blue balls since the moment I clapped eyes on you because I only want you."

"Less talking, wolf. More action." Jasmine reached for his belt, and Roman moved out of reach.

"I thought you wanted me to talk dirty to you, Jazz. Don't you want me to make you come against my mouth?"

Jasmine lay back on the bed and groaned, her hips arching upward. Roman gripped her hip with one hand, then stripped off her pants and panties, leaving her gloriously naked on the bed beneath him. His hands gripped her thighs, spreading them slightly as he glanced down at her core like it was dessert. Setting his knee on the bed, he pulled her core down. The harsh fabric of his jeans against her most intimate part wrung a cry from her.

Roman lowered his mouth to her right breast, cupping the left and pressing his thumb hard on the nipple as he sucked the other in his mouth. When Jasmine gasped, he increased the pressure until she was lifting her hips and the sensations made her cry out.

"Roman."

His name came out of her mouth in a breathy rush, lifting up so that he would kiss her. He shifted his knee as he kissed her, palming her breast until her hands went to his shoulders and she scored his back with her nails.

With a grin, Roman broke the kiss, catching her hands as she tried to reach for his belt. "If you free my cock, then I'm going to be inside you. Don't you want me to see if I can live up to the vision?"

"Oh gods, yes. Now, Roman."

He chuckled at the order in her tone, leaning in to bite at her pulse. "I think I like having you give me orders. We can do that later. But now, I have to have a taste."

Roman wanted to tease her, felt her skin flush under his touch, his lips tracing down her sternum, then to her hip as he backed off the bed, his feet touching the floor. He kissed and nipped his way along the inside of her thigh, encouraged at the mewling sounds she was making.

Roman dropped to his knees, his hands on her ankles, and he gave a sharp tug, bringing Jasmine's slick wetness to eye level. He growled his approval, easing back to admire what he was about to finally do with his tongue, his mouth.

"Roman, dear gods, do something, anything. My body's on fire. I need to … I need to …"

He didn't give her a chance to finish what she wanted to say. Instead, Roman gripped her thighs, spread them a little wider, and then he lunged, licking at her core with a growl. Jasmine writhed as he plunged his tongue in and out of her honeyed core. It was like a little slice of heaven, having her push against his mouth, and as he glanced up to see her back arched, her fingers gripping the sheets, he inserted a finger, stroking in and out as he sucked.

Jasmine moaned, shuddering as Roman ate at her like she was dinner and dessert all rolled into one, adding a second finger, his own heart hammering in his chest, his cock pressed painfully against the seam of his jeans. But he did not stop his relentless task, felt the tremors beginning to build in Jasmine as she thrust her hips once, twice, and then she came apart, shouting his name.

Roman kept stroking her through her orgasm, easing her gently as he watched her come down, and she lay there, all flushed and sweaty. Roman slowly eased his fingers out of

Jasmine, her body shuddering as he did, then he crawled onto the bed, kissing Jasmine's throat as he pulled her into his arms, her head resting on his chest. He stroked his hand down her body, resting it on the curve of her ass.

"That was … I mean …"

Roman laughed as Jasmine found it hard to verbalize her feelings. She lifted her head, and he kissed her, trying to keep himself from sinking into the kiss even more.

Jasmine yawned as the sun rose outside the window, her fingertips trailing across his chest. "That was way better than the vision. I want to do that again."

She yawned again, snuggling into his chest, throwing a leg over his as she muttered, "I want to make you come."

"We have plenty of time, darling. Sleep now. I'm sure the wolf will still be hungry after you've slept."

Jasmine was already half asleep as she mumbled, "She said you'd be the death of me, wolf. Maybe I should have listened."

Roman went to ask her what she meant, but Jasmine was already asleep as his heart raced and the blissed-out feeling that he had just felt vanished.

What the hell had she meant by him being the death of her?

CHAPTER TWELVE

Jasmine

JASMINE WOKE HOURS LATER, STRETCHING FOR A SECOND BEFORE she froze, realizing that she was naked and that she was plastered all over a half-dressed Roman. The wolf's eyes were closed, his chest rising up and down. She straddled his thighs, the wolf's palm resting on the curve of her butt, his other hand around her shoulders.

Jasmine had always considered that Dylan had been exaggerating when he told her how fun and how hot sex was, knowing her brother's experience far exceeded hers, but last night, when Roman went down on her with a steely focus, she had come apart harder than she had in her lifetime.

He had been relentless, making sure that she knew he didn't see her as Duke saw her, and he had held back from getting his own pleasure to make sure she was happy.

The prophetess will lose herself to a wolf like no other.

It will either be her end or her awakening.

And of course, Roman was a wolf like no other, one who could not shift. She felt her heart cracking open, but she could not risk it because she didn't want to take the chance that falling for Roman would mean certain death for her.

Jasmine took advantage of the fact that Roman was still sleeping to trace her fingertips along his muscular chest, along the puckered scarring, brushing her knuckles along his beard and the feel of it, rough as it had been against the skin in between her legs. She quivered at the reminder of it.

Dancing her fingers along his sternum, feeling the rise of his chest, Jasmine dropped her gaze to the dark dusting of hair that trailed from his belly button and disappeared into his jeans. Her hand dipped lower, Jasmine now aware that Roman's breathing had changed, so she moved her fingers back up to his chest, where a low rumble emanated.

"Oh my god, did you just purr?"

"Wolves don't purr. But you can keep on petting me if you like. I can grin and bear it."

Jasmine laughed, lifting her upper body as Roman slid his hand to the nape of her neck and kissed her gently. Her body instantly flushed with heat, shifting so that the material on his jeans rubbed her core, and she wanted Roman to use that talented tongue of his again.

"Jazz."

By all that was holy, the way Roman said her name, like it was a prayer and a penance all at once, made her brave. She dragged her lips from his, feathering kisses down his jaw, neck, along his collarbone, and then swallowed down her reservations and pressed an open-mouth kiss to his pecs. The sound of Roman's growl sent a shudder right down to her toes.

She repeated the action, this time sliding her hand down to cup his erection through his jeans. Roman's hips jerked at the contact, the wolf swearing as Jasmine scraped her teeth down his nipple.

"Fuck me." Roman cursed again as Jasmine smiled against his skin.

Jasmine boldly rubbed her palm up and down twice more before Roman pounced on her. Suddenly she was on her back, a giggle slipping free of her lips, and then she clasped a hand over her mouth, felt her eyes widen even as Roman grinned.

His eyes burned with heat as he lowered his head. Jasmine's body sparked with anticipation as her phone blared. They both looked to where Roman had dropped her pants, ignored it, then the bloody thing started ringing again, and Roman blew out a frustrated breath and rolled off her.

Jasmine crouched down to pluck her phone from her pocket, sneaking a peek over her shoulder to see Roman's eyes focused on her. The phone started ringing again, and with a sigh, she pressed the answer button.

"This better be life and death, or I will find you and kill you."

"Well damn, Liam Neeson, calm down."

Jasmine rolled her eyes. "You're not supposed to be calling me, Dylan."

She heard her brother sigh down the phone. "I know, I know. The fates want to kill me and all that BS. What I can't stand is my baby sister waking from a fucking coma and then getting the hell out of dodge without even a text? For fuck sake, Jazz."

Jasmine reached down and pulled on Roman's tee, not the one he loaned her but the one he had been wearing, feeling too vulnerable to be naked while Dylan yelled at her. She sat down at the edge of the bed. "I already lost one brother by ignoring a vision, you idiot. I couldn't lose you because I wanted a hug."

There was a moment of silence, then Dylan swore. "Well now I feel like a dick, but I can make it up to you. Check your phone."

Her phone vibrated. Jasmine clicked on the encrypted link that opened the assassin app to see a familiar face flash on the screen, and she sucked in a breath.

"Don't ever say I never give you anything nice."

Jasmine didn't bother to hide her smile, knowing Dylan would hear it in her voice. "You do give great gifts, bro. Now tell me what I need to know."

"Silas popped up at some of the less classy establishments asking where he could get his hands on some children that no one would miss. We've been after Silas for over thirty years,

Jazz. Since he gave you the slip. One of our assassins recognised him, knew you had called it, set up a meet for tonight with a broker."

"That makes me the broker, I guess," she confirmed with Dylan.

Silas had been a hench warlock for the mission she had gone on thirty years ago, and he had managed to slip away before Jasmine could kill him, but she had taken out his boss, the warlock who called himself Vincenzo. That was just before she had crossed paths with the seer who told her of her tangled fate with a wolf.

Silas had continued to harvest bones from children for magic, and Jasmine wanted nothing more than to kill him. It had been a mistake on her part, stopping to listen to the seer while chasing down Silas, but she would not let this opportunity pass her by.

"Who is he expecting?" she asked Dylan.

"Olivia Lemuel."

Well damn, that meant Jasmine would need her kit, which meant going home to Sicarius, and like hell if she wasn't confused as to why she felt a sense of loss already at having to leave the cabin, especially when all she wanted to do was get Roman as naked as she had been.

"Dylan …" Jasmine started, but her brother cut her off.

"I know, I know. I'm already headed to Dante's to pull a shift so you can come back and get into character mode. Silas is expecting you and your bodyguard at Le Clerc's at 2 a.m. If Roman doesn't want to play assassin's bodyguard, then let me know and I'll send Izzy."

Jasmine looked over her shoulder, knowing full well Roman heard what had been said, yet it still surprised her when he bopped his head and rolled out of the bed, heading for the shower. Jasmine waited until she heard the water running before she began speaking again.

"How much does Roman know about the side gig?"

"Everything," Dylan answered. "When you were knocked out and we were looking into who this Vindicta dude might be, we had to look into your old assassin kills. So he got an intimate look into the work we do in public and in private."

"And what did he say?" Jasmine's voice was nothing more than a whisper, and she was certain that if her heart could beat, it would be drumming inside her chest right now.

"He sat down with my tablet, and after an hour he lifted his head, having studied the files way more than I ever have, and said it was a lucrative idea to make a little money from killing sick bastards. Didn't see the difference in him getting paid to kill terrorists by private contracts and you killing child-killers."

Jasmine couldn't help but think of Duke, who had come very close to striking her when she had come home one night, covered in a mark's blood, after he had specifically ordered her not to do it in the first place. Duke wanted to shape her into his ideal image of a vampire mate, while Roman had done nothing but support Jasmine and stand up for her.

"Roman isn't Colin, Jazz," Dylan said softly, and Jasmine laughed.

"You a mind reader now as well, bro?"

A car door closed, and Jasmine heard an engine start up. "Nope, I'll leave that to our glorious Primus. I'm headed out, Jazz. I'll see you in a few days, and be careful of Silas. He knows how badly you want him dead. Love ya."

Dylan hung up before she could say it back. Jasmine shook her head as she debated joining Roman in the shower but knew if they started it, they would soon be back in the tumble of sheets. She ducked out of the room and went to the shower in the communal bathroom, quickly showering and changing into tracksuit bottoms and a hoodie, not caring what she was wearing because becoming Olivia Lemuel was a process that would happen at home.

Roman was gazing out the window eating a sandwich as

she stepped into the kitchen area. He nodded at the wrapped sandwich he had made for her on the table. "For the road."

There was a thick tension in the air that wasn't there before. Roman's shoulders were stiff, his tone brooding. Jasmine took the sandwich as Roman came over to grab his keys, and Jasmine inhaled his scent, smelling like the forest around them.

Roman leaned across her to grab his phone and wallet, so Jasmine leaned up and pressed her lips to his cheek, much to the wolf's surprise.

"What was that for?"

Jasmine shrugged her shoulders with a wry smile. "Just 'cause."

That tiny interaction seemed to loosen whatever knot was in Roman as his lips curved into a slow, deliberate smile that infuriatingly made her stomach and other places clench.

Jasmine headed for the door, not bothering to look over her shoulder because she could feel the weight of Roman's gaze on her. The car journey was filled with a simmering kind of anticipation as Jasmine ate her sandwich, not because she was hungry but because Roman made it for her.

When they arrived at Sicarius Security, Roman drove down to the underground car park and pulled into a free space. But he didn't get out of the car.

"I'm only there as the muscle tonight. This is all you. Be careful. We will be finishing what you started this morning."

That was all Roman said as he got out of the car, then strode around to open Jasmine's door for her. She rolled her eyes but still smiled as they headed for the elevator, Roman's hand on the small of her back. Checking her phone, she saw that they had a few hours before the meet, so Jasmine pressed the button for the family floor.

The doors opened as her family was just readying for breakfast. Though after six, and normally long after Malakai would have been at his desk, her brother was dressed in grey tracksuit bottoms and sleeveless tee. Keeva was nursing a coffee as she glanced up, looking from Jasmine to the closeness of Roman to her.

Malakai turned, offering a broad smile as she heard her name, and turned toward the couch. Scarlett Russell hoisted herself up and came toward Jasmine in what could only be described as a waddle, her rounded belly looking like it was about to burst.

Scarlett glowed with happiness as she hugged Jasmine, the reluctant succubus having found her strength when she fell for Jazz's adopted brother Zeke, who now had an instant family after years of self-hatred and darkness.

Obscurum.

Shaking the thought away, Jasmine stepped out of the embrace as she saw Scarlett's eyes flash a deeper shade of blue. The succubus licked her lips, her eyes widening at whatever she was sensing from Jasmine.

"Where's Zeke?"

The entire room fell silent as Scarlett worried at her lip, and it was only Keeva's smirk that stopped Jasmine from thinking that Zeke had slipped back to old habits. Zeke had spent a lot of time hating what he had become, believing God had cursed him and made him a monster, and it had taken Scarlett to finally have him accept himself.

It was still hard though.

Hands on her hips, Jasmine raised her brows. "Okay, someone spill. Where is Zeke?"

"Dumbass is hiding from Scarlett," Keeva said, laughter in her tone.

Jasmine watched Scarlett blush a furious shade of red, even as tears filled her eyes. She cupped Scarlett's cheek. "Why is the idiot hiding?"

"Oh god, this is so embarrassing." Scarlett groaned as she slid her gaze to Keeva, Scarlett's best friend, who was trying and failing miserably to hold back her laughter.

"It seems that Ezekiel," Malakai began with a bemused smile, "has gotten it into his head that he may hurt little Grayce when he and Scarlett are intimate."

It took a second for Jasmine's brain to catch up as Scarlett went even redder, Keeva just about busting a gut at how hilarious it sounded. Jasmine looked at Malakai, who shrugged.

"It appears he read an article that sex during the last trimester while the baby was aware may be alarming. And since Scarlett is a succubus and needs sex to survive, and her … appetite has grown during pregnancy, Zeke has been hiding in his library."

A fat tear slipped free of Scarlett's eye as the succubus said, "I know he doesn't think I'm attractive, looking all fat and all, but I never wanted to make him hide away in the library."

Roman strode over and wrapped Scarlett in a hug.

"Oh god, you smell good." The succubus groaned before she clasped a hand over her mouth, relaxing only when Roman winked at her and said, "Please don't say that in front of your man. I like my balls where they are."

That made Scarlett snort with laughter as Jasmine headed toward the library. The moment she opened the door, she heard the soft rock and nearly let out a sigh in relief, knowing Zeke tormented himself by only listening to classical music when he was in a really bad place.

Jasmine climbed the stairs and then glanced around Zeke's library, her mind travelling back to when they had first acquired this building, had started to mould it into the home and security they had not had in centuries and Jasmine had tried to get Zeke involved in sorting the library.

"Jazz, catch."

Dylan tossed the heavy tome in Jasmine's direction. She ducked with a shriek, bracing herself for the bang that came when the book crashed to the floor, but it never came. Jasmine turned to see Ezekiel standing at the bottom of the steps, his face grim and his eyes as black as they had been since the day fate had sent her to him.

He folded his arms across his chest, after setting the book down on one of the various trolleys that held the books needed for sorting. Shaking his head, he looked at Jasmine and Dylan before he began speaking.

"Have you both no respect for books?"

Dylan held up his hands in slight apology. "You know, if you helped out and actually took an interest, then us heathens might just pay a little bit more care and attention to the dead trees."

Dylan tossed an original copy of James Joyce's Ulysses into the air as Zeke growled and stalked forward to catch it before it, too, landed on the ground. Zeke nudged Dylan by grabbing his head and pushing him toward the steps.

"Get out. I can do this."

Delight flooded through Jasmine as Dylan winked, his eyes bleeding red for a second as he took some of Zeke's anger into himself and left Jasmine to corral their newest kin.

"You can go too, Jasmine. I am used to my own company."

"But you don't have to walk the path alone, Zeke. You have us now. But this is your library, so I can just help you." She rolled up the sleeves of her shirt. "So put me to work."

And so, for a few hours, from dusk unto dawn, they worked in relative silence, putting books on shelves, Jasmine nodding eagerly as Zeke pointed out books that Jasmine might find interesting or ones Malakai could take a look at. Slowly, the library took form, became warmer, and Zeke had sought refuge in it for decades to come.

Jasmine jogged down the steps, headed straight for the alcove where Zeke had slumbered until he had hooked up with Scarlett, and found her vampire brother drinking a large glass of whiskey.

"Dude, it's got to be big if you are hitting the hard stuff."

Zeke grunted in greeting, reached into his drawer at his desk and pulled out a glass, filling it with just a sliver, then slid it to Jasmine. She took the glass and a drink before setting the glass down on the table.

"You know she thinks you don't find her attractive because she's the size of a small country, right? Or are you just that dense?"

Zeke's gaze snapped up. "That is so not the fucking issue."

"Then what is?"

Scrubbing a hand down his face, scratching at the stubble on his chin, Zeke sighed. "The baby is active. She feels things, according to Dylan. What if she feels us ... you know?"

Zeke looked so earnest that Jasmine couldn't even laugh. "I don't know from personal experience, but I swear that Grayce has no idea what's going on. I'm pretty sure you two are good."

"Okay. But ... fucking hell ... this is not the conversation I want to have with my sister."

And just that sentence gave Jasmine a case of the warm fuzzies.

"You want to talk to Dylan? He is the sexpert."

Zeke shook his head, then closed his eyes and just blurted out, "I'm worried the sex is too much. Scarlett can't control her powers when we ... dammit." He growled, banging his head off the table.

"So basically, Scarlett lets her power out and you can't ... um, you can't keep it vanilla?"

CHAPTER THIRTEEN

Jasmine

"Ya, that about sums it up. Christ, this is ..."

"Totally normal when you are in love with a succubus."

Zeke barked out a laugh that sounded strangled. "If you had told me, even a couple of years ago, that we would be having this discussion, I would have thought you crazy."

Jasmine sighed. "Listen, Zeke. Scarlett is worried about Grayce. She's worried about you. Her hormones are probably all over the place, and she needs you. While I totally don't want the deets on my brothers' sex lives, you gotta talk to her. Hiding away in your library won't help either of you."

Jasmine held out her hand, waited until Zeke drained his drink, then he took her hand, got to his feet, and walked out with her. They emerged from the library to the sound of Scarlett's laughter, which eased some of the tension in Zeke's frame.

The succubus was leaning against the breakfast counter, watching as Keeva and Roman arm-wrestled. Keeva had already begun sweating, her face drawn in a firm line of concentration as Roman had a sly turn of his lips. Keeva barked out another curse as Roman applied a little pressure.

Scarlett turned toward them, as if she had sensed Zeke's presence, self-doubt immediately flooding her eyes. The activity in the room halted as Zeke stepped forward, as Scarlett moved towards him. Scarlett's hand fell to her stomach as

Zeke took Scarlett's face in his hands and then kissed the ever-loving hell out of her.

Jasmine grinned as Scarlett nearly melted, and then Zeke was dragging her to the lift, and they all saw the couple kiss again before the doors closed.

Jasmine stayed for a few minutes, then gave Malakai and Keeva a quick hug and headed for the lift herself with Roman in tow. They didn't say anything in the elevator. Jasmine was glad of the few minutes to gather herself.

Normally, before a job, she had a process. A way of shedding Jasmine and becoming whoever she was for the night. Sharing this with Roman, showing him this side of her, felt strangely more intimate than getting naked with him had been. Roman knew she was an assassin, had seen her fight, yet this part of her process was not something she had shared with anyone.

When the elevator arrived at her floor, Jasmine stepped inside and glanced around her room. It was hideously pink, and she loved it. The walls, the carpet, the four-poster canopy bed. She had chosen to go all out because it was one of the first big choices she had to make for herself. She had been younger then, and perhaps she was due for an overhaul.

This isn't appropriate for a couple.

Jasmine shook her head to banish the thought from her mind, to push the images of Roman and his stuff in her rooms, in her bed. She needed to concentrate right now, and thinking of Roman naked in her bed would not make her focus.

"You can wait upstairs with Malakai and Keeva if you like. This will take a few minutes."

"Nah, I'm good," came his response.

Jasmine gestured to the kitchenette area, then strode into her closet. She felt Roman standing in the doorway as she moved a bunch of DKNY and Dolce dresses aside to reveal a panel with a keypad. Glancing over her shoulder, she held

Roman's gaze. "I suppose it's useless asking you to give me a minute."

"Ask me and see what I say."

Rolling her eyes, Jasmine folded her arms across her chest. "I've never let another person in this room. Not even Dylan or Malakai. So don't touch anything and don't annoy me."

Jasmine pressed the keypad with her passcode, then waited as a panel slid up and she put her eye to it. Roman almost jumped out of his skin when a voice sounded.

"Good evening, Jasmine. Access granted."

"Thank you, Sicarius. Admit two, please."

The heavy door whirled as the lock disengaged, and then it slid across the back of her wardrobe and she stepped inside. The lights came on in a burst of three, illuminating Jasmine's collection as she heard Roman mutter, "Fucking hell." Then he whistled.

From left to right, the hideaway held all the tools she needed to change her appearance. She had a section for clothes and shoes, a section for wigs, and a section for colour-changing contacts. There were accessories that were custom-made and had weapons built into them. On the back wall, Jasmine had a variety of actual weapons, from a bow and arrow to knives to guns and even a sword.

Roman strode around the room, his eyes taking every-thing in, his face unreadable as he reached out to touch her sword, then pulled back his hand like he just remembered she had told him not to touch anything. Then he turned slowly to face her.

"This is something else."

"I know," she answered smugly, earning a chuckle. "Jasmine Cavanagh can't go around killing bad people. I mean, every assassin has their own methods, but I became another persona, and this is how I do it."

Jasmine walked around the room, searching for what she needed to become Olivia Lemuel. Jasmine had used that identity for seven years since she read the book series *Midnight, Texas* and had mashed two characters' names together in a hurry when she needed to pretend to be a broker who could acquire what others could not.

Most Inferna hated paranormal books, so it would take someone to admit that they read it to pick holes in her identity, especially since Olivia Lemuel already had a very extensive history if anyone ran a background check on her. Dylan made sure that all her various personas were iron-clad if anyone decided to have a nose around.

She selected a lilac-coloured wig, took it down from the shelf on the head-stand, and set it down on the vanity table in the centre of the room. Jasmine was conscious that Roman was watching her and felt a wave of unease in her chest, so she started to get organized, ruffled by the audience of her transformation.

Separating her long hair into three sections, Jasmine began the process of braiding those three separate sections, similar to the way she used to braid it back when she was human. "Most movies get it wrong when they think using a wig is easy. I mean, they throw those on and off like it's nothing. But it actually takes more than that."

When her hair was braided, she opened up one of the drawers and pulled out some hairpins. She wrapped the first braid on her right around the back of her head and then used the pins to secure the hair in place, repeating with the second, but in the opposite direction, and then the final coming straight up the back, using a few more pins to secure the braids in place.

Stealing a glance at Roman, she saw the wolf watching her with a sharp, intense focus. Jasmine opened another drawer and pulled out her wig cap. It looked like fishnet stockings, but for someone with as much hair as she had, over the years, Jasmine found these just worked better for her.

She pulled it on over her head and pulled the thicker end

over, tucking the extra material under the back, and secured it with another pin. She then pulled out a velvet band that looked like a hairband and placed it over the front of her hairline, adding another pin or two, and satisfied with the look, she got up.

And still Roman watched her, probably wondering why she wasn't putting the wig on yet.

She selected a dark purple set of lenses and put them in. Her eyes burned as she did so, but after blinking a few times, she got used to it. By the time she was sitting back to apply her makeup, she could almost forget they were there. Jasmine moved her chair slightly to the right, opening up the table and using some makeup to darken her skin a little, using a dark shadow to make her eyes smaller. Then she used a black colour on her lips. Of all the parts, the makeup was probably the easiest, but it could make or break the final look, and so as with everything, she was meticulous with the details.

Makeup and lenses in place, with a grin, she reached out for the lilac-coloured wig, running her hand through the hair. She threw it over and settled the wig over her head, just up to the velvet band. The inbuilt combs she pushed into place, sliding them under the headband at the front, and then slid the comb at the back in place. She brushed the wig to settle it more, having pulled it in place. Just in case she had to move about a little more, if Silas put up a fight, she used some more pins just above her ears to hold the wig in place.

"Olivia Lemuel is a high-level broker who can get you anything your heart desires. She is also a cold-hearted bitch with a penchant for expensive things. Last time, Isolde came as my bodyguard. You just have to stand there and look menacing. I'll do the rest."

Roman didn't answer her, simply nodded. Jasmine picked a bat-shaped choker from her assemble, knowing the metal that would rest in her neck came apart with a flick, and the bat-shaped ears were laced with the venom of a snake shifter.

Dylan always had the best gifts.

Jasmine stripped out of her clothes, feeling a swell of smug satisfaction at the rumble from Roman as she stood there in just her bra and panties. She pulled on black jeans that looked like there was no way in hell she could move in them, yet they were made of a Lycra material that meant she could look good and still kick ass. She grabbed a black vest top, which she pulled on and tucked it into the waist of the jeans, tightening the leather belt attached to it. Reaching into her discarded jacket, she fished out her karambits and sheathed them into the hidden strap in the back of the belt.

She pulled out a dark purple, leather-look jacket and slipped it on as she stepped into heels that made her nearly as tall as Roman. She strapped two wristlets to her wrists, the coolness of the blades concealed in them kissing her skin.

When she turned in Roman's direction, the wolf was watching her with hungry eyes, the same expression that most men got when they looked at Olivia Lemuel. She joked to Roman about a wild night with Olivia, saying it off the cuff but surprised that she was a little bitter that the wolf was looking at her like she was a snack. She was even more surprised by his next words.

"I can't deny that your ass looks superb in those pants," Roman admitted as strode forward, gripping her chin with his thumb and finger to keep her eyes on him. "And I'm all for a little dress-up fun, but I know the woman who is underneath all that disguise. The other men don't know her. And thank fuck for that. They can ogle Olivia Lemuel all they want. It's Jasmine Cavanagh that I want all to myself."

Roman strode from the room then, citing his need to get a vehicle suitable for Olivia Lemuel. Jasmine took a few seconds to mull over what Roman had said, the fact he had said he wanted her, not so much the fantasy, and she felt another chip appear in the wall around her heart.

She fastened a gun to her hip, Olivia's usual weapon of

choice, then headed out to her bedroom, grabbing her phone as she heard it vibrate with a message from Roman telling her to meet him in the car park.

Jasmine made her way down in the elevator. The door opened, and she stepped into the dimly lit lot to see Roman sticking fake plates onto Zeke's Mercedes. The wolf had changed himself as well, wearing tactical pants and a black tee that was no doubt made with a Kevlar so thin you wouldn't know the difference, yet it was nearly impenetrable.

A black bomber jacket finished his ensemble, and though she could see no visible weapons, there was no doubt the wolf was armed to the hilt. Roman rose to his full height with a grin, opened the back door of the car and then, after she had ducked inside, he got into the driver's side and they headed out.

"We need a code word. In case you need me to intervene."

"I won't," came her answer, and she shocked herself at the defensive tone.

"Isolde gave me the plates. Told me that you always have a code word. Don't treat me as less of an asset, Jasmine. Tonight, I'm there to take a bullet for you if you need it."

"It won't come to that." Jasmine held up a little vial so Roman could see it in the mirror. "I slip that in his drink, and Silas will be dead. Nothing to tie Olivia to it. But if you want to use a code word, then okay. Commando. That's the code word."

Roman just rolled his eyes and they drove into the city, heading for the more upmarket side of the city, where the richest of Inferna and humans liked to dine. Le Clerc's used to be a dingy nightclub, but the vampire who owned it changed it to a high-end brothel. Money was no good at Le Clerc's; you bought your fantasies with a piece of your soul, a sliver of magic, or a lifetime of servitude.

Roman pulled up to the valet, got out of the car, and handed him a fifty to look after the car. Then Roman glanced from left to right and opened her door, holding out his arm for her to take. Jasmine got out of the car, jerked her chin up like she was an important SOB, and headed for the door of Le Clerc's.

Jasmine had been to Paris a few times, had dined in expensive restaurants, and Le Clerc's appeared as extensively expensive as they did. Golden chandeliers hung from the ceiling, ambient French classical music filling the room. She offered her name to the person manning the door. His eyes widened, but then he quickly ushered her through the main dining area to the cigar room.

Smoking indoors was banned in Ireland, but that never stopped the Inferna. With Roman at her back, they crossed into the cigar room, the heady scent of smoke and sweat hitting her. Jasmine looked around, spotting Silas, anticipation in her veins as her mark turned to look at her, the moment he felt the weight of her gaze on him.

Getting to his feet as she sashayed toward him, Silas looked just as he had when she had killed his mentor and he had slipped out of her grasp. Small in stature, Silas was bulky, with a rounded belly and beady eyes. His dark hair hung in waves down to his shoulders, his beard concealing his face and the scar she had given him the last time they met.

Silas reached for her hand, lifting the back to his lips as he smirked at her. "Olivia Lemuel. It is an honour to meet you."

Jasmine withdrew her hand. "I heard you have something you want me to acquire."

Silas looked from her to Roman, then waved him away. "Send the guard dog away, Ms. Lemuel. Then you and I can have a drink without prying eyes."

"My patrons and clients worry for my safety. They require me to have someone who can look mean and dissuade anyone from trying to cross me."

Silas offered her a seat, which she took, waiting as Silas ordered champagne for them both, some expensive shit that cost nearly a hundred euros a glass, and it was all so Silas could show he had money.

"I have a few things that need to be retrieved, and the person I work for is willing to pay a small fortune to the person who gets him what he needs."

Jasmine rolled her eyes. "I don't work by proxy, Silas. I am the intermediary. I deal with the organ grinder, not the monkey."

Silas bristled at her tone, taking a sip of his champagne. "Olivia, can I call you Olivia?" he asked but didn't wait for her to answer before he continued. "My acquaintance has people hunting for him; therefore, he simply cannot move about freely. Let me tell you what we need, and then you can decide if you are up to the task. Perhaps a show of your skills would garner a face-to-face."

Silas reached over and placed his palm on her calf, and as Roman growled, tearing Silas's attention from her, Jasmine pulled out a needle from her wristlet and stabbed it into his knuckle. Silas howled, but no one seemed to bat an eyelid as he yanked his hand to his chest.

"You don't get to touch me, Silas. Next time you do, you'll find yourself with a Prince Albert."

Silas turned to the waiter and asked for something for his hand as Jasmine deftly uncorked the vial and tipped the contents into Silas's glass before warlock turned back. When he did, he immediately took a large drink from the glass.

Excellent.

"The person who hired me asked to gather the bones of a child who died before taking a breath, the scale of a dragon, the dust from a unicorn's horn." Silas listed a few things that were common in spells, and that was when what Silas was looking for became suddenly interesting.

"He is looking for the lost pages of the book of Lucifer. And he also is looking for the remnants of Michael's sword, and lastly, he wanted to know if you had anyone on the payroll with the ability to sneak undetected into any building?"

The lost pages of the book of Lucifer were tucked in a vault in Zeke's library, the vampire having found them many years ago in his quest to understand who and what he was. But why would he need someone to get into any building?

"I have someone who has managed get herself into the most secure building in the world undetected. Another mere building should be easy, but costly."

Keeva had used her smarts and a flaw in Dylan's security to get into Sicarius and almost kill Malakai. Had her brother not been impervious to Keeva's kiss of death, she may have succeeded instead of falling for him.

Silas smiled, and it was that smarmy smirk that crawled over her skin. "Good, then we need her to do it again. My employer requires her to either capture the succubus and bring her to him or wait until she gives birth and bring him the infant."

Jesus, Mary and Joseph and the fucking wee donkey: Silas was working for Vindicta!

CHAPTER FOURTEEN

Roman

THE BASTARD HAD JUST OPENLY TOLD THEM THAT THEY WANTED to hurt Scarlett and the baby.

Roman betrayed none of the emotions running through him as Jasmine calmly laughed, then remarked, "Your boss better have deep pockets if he wants me to have one of my crew kidnap the infant."

"He is willing to write you a blank cheque," Silas confirmed, his eyes roaming over Jasmine in a pervy way that made Roman's wolf snarl and paw at the inside of his mind.

Dammit, the asshole wanted to get his hands on Ezekiel and Scarlett's baby at any cost. Jasmine tapped her fingers to her chin like she was mulling over the proposal, then tilted her head.

"If I am to face the wrath of the Primus and his considerable reach, and I can deliver what your boss wants, then I need a face-to-face arranged. I won't deal with you when my neck is on the line."

Silas drained his drink, not knowing he now only had maybe an hour before the toxin worked its way through his system, his organs failing and pain riddling his body. He also didn't realise how badly Jasmine wanted to hang around and watch, but she had to be long out of dodge before he started feeling ill.

"I think that can be arranged. But let us get a room, Olivia.

We can talk in private, and perhaps I could indulge in a fantasy of mine."

Jasmine chuckled, shaking her head. "No thanks, warlock. I know your reputation. Besides, I like my men a little more rough and ready." Jasmine slid her gaze to Roman, then back to Silas, whose jaw was clenched to show how pissed he was that she had turned him down for the help.

"Jasmine?"

You have got to be fucking kidding me!

Of all the vampires to be in Le Clerc's tonight and, it had to be Jasmine's absolute bell-end of an ex. He was dressed in an old-fashioned suit, the kind you would see in some period drama or some shit, his eyes wide, his contempt at seeing Jasmine written all over his face. Roman considered this as he would have thought for someone who managed to convince Jasmine he had loved her, someone who was able to fool Malakai, that they would be able to school their expressions a bit more.

And Roman wanted to punch him in the teeth if it meant it would shut the fool up.

Jasmine's head snapped round at the sound of a familiar voice, as Roman blocked Colin from coming any closer. Roman glared at Colin Thorpe, the idiot who had shattered Jasmine's confidence.

"You have the wrong person, vampire. Enjoy your night."

Colin laughed, a bitter sound, as Roman grabbed his arm and yanked him a little back. "You heard the lady. You have the wrong fucking person."

Colin shook off Roman's hand, Roman holding on for a second or two longer than necessary. "How can you stand to see her in all that fakeness? She shames her Kiss by pretending to be someone important when really, she is just going out and killing. No female should be this at home with death. Silas, she is a fraud."

Silas was already on his feet as Jasmine unleashed a blade

and held it to the warlock's neck. "Well, damn. I actually liked this alias. Never mind, I kinda wanted you to know that it was me that killed you."

Silas sucked in a breath as it dawned on him just exactly who she was. "Jasmine … as in Jasmine Cavanagh."

"In the flesh." Jasmine flicked the hair of her wig off her shoulder, a frequent Jasmine gesture, as Silas bristled.

Roman fought a grin at the flippant tone Jasmine used, taking a step forward in the hopes of halting Colin from aiding his warlock friend. But just how involved was he in Vindicta's plans? Was his being here really a coincidence, or was Colin more involved than anyone suspected? Definitely something that needed more investigation, but for now Roman focused on the issue in front of him.

"Does my brother know that you are on friendly terms with the enemy, Colin?" Jasmine asked as she peered at Colin, no hint of any affection in her eyes for her ex, as if she was finally getting past what he had made her feel or think about herself.

Colin didn't get a chance to answer because Silas jerked back, pulling a bag from his pocket and tossing it into the air, muttering a spell. The bag burst into flames, and the spell weaved its way into the room. Patrons started fighting one another as Jasmine lunged for Silas.

Roman wanted to help her, but he sensed the fist coming for him and ducked, leaving Colin to stumble forward. Roman grabbed him in a headlock as Jasmine fought with Silas. Colin struggled in his grasp, but unlike someone who was alive, the headlock didn't subdue him. The little bitch sank his fangs into Roman's arm.

Roman let him go and shoved him away, not even glancing at the marks left on his arm. Colin spat Roman's blood on the ground, and Roman ducked as a chair flew through the air.

"I can smell her on you," Thorpe taunted him, sniffing at

him like he had no manners. He cast his eyes over Roman, inspecting him, but Roman didn't even flinch as Colin spat out his words. "What makes you think you can succeed where I failed? What makes you think you can break her in, curb that foul tongue of hers?"

Roman chortled, shaking his head. "You're a fucking idiot. I don't want to break her; I want to watch her grow. You didn't deserve her."

The sneer on Colin's face was ugly. "And you do?"

"No, I don't, but that means I will work twice as hard to be worthy of her."

It was the god's honest truth as Roman pulled out his gun and shot Colin square in the chest. The vampire howled as he clutched at his chest.

"You shot me!" Colin shrilled like the whiny bitch he was.

Roman grabbed him by the collar and leaned in to whisper, relishing the widening of Thorpe's eyes in complete shock as Roman said, "Just be lucky it's not laced with gold."

Then Roman punched him. The vampire hit the ground as Roman simply stepped over the unconscious idiot and caught Silas as Jasmine tossed him toward Roman, who grabbed the warlock and held him in place. Jasmine glanced down at the talisman of bones around the warlock's neck and yanked it clean off him, the scent of magic slowly evaporating as Jasmine dropped it to the ground and crushed the fragile bones with her foot, causing the warlock to hiss.

Jasmine lifted her blade to Silas's throat, her grin wicked. "I knew I would find you eventually. I knew you would look into my eyes and know that the scar I gave you is nothing compared with the poison now in your veins. Your organs will bubble and burn until they burst, and you will die in excruciating pain, pain like you inflicted on those kids."

Silas's eyes opened wide, sweat beading on his forehead. "He would have killed me anyway, now that I made a mistake and told you what he needs."

"Tell me what his plans are? Help me and maybe it can be a little redemption." Jasmine offered him more than Roman would have, a chance to go to his death with a little peace.

Silas chortled, shrugging against Roman's hold. "I know where I go when I die. But when the world is remade anew, I will rise to serve him, and I will come for you and the wolf. Then I will watch you both bleed."

Silas surged forward, impaling himself on Jasmine's blade, and severing his carotid artery. Roman let Silas go, blood gushing from his neck, the life draining from his eyes before he collapsed on the ground. Jasmine glanced down at him, then lifted her gaze to Roman.

"For fuck sake … I could have totally saved the poison. That shit is expensive."

Roman chuckled, shaking his head, then he pointed to Colin. "What are we gonna do with this douchebag?"

Jasmine's smile should have chilled his bones, but it only ignited the flames in him.

"Oh, Malakai will be wanting a word with him. I'll call for a pickup."

Jasmine pulled out her phone and began talking to Malakai, telling him what had happened, as Roman glanced around to see that the bar had emptied out, leaving a wave of destruction in their wake. Tables were smashed, chairs were broken, and the scent of blood was in the air. Roman bent down and hoisted Colin over his shoulder, following Jasmine out after she motioned for him to follow her as she continued to talk down the phone.

Once out in the night air, Roman called for the car and set Colin down on the ground, not caring when the vampire slid and hit his head on the concrete. Jasmine had walked to the middle of the road as if she were looking for something.

At this time of night, the roads were empty, with no traffic on the road with people that would wonder why there was a woman just standing in the middle it.

"Kai, Silas made it sound like they had tried to get into Sicarius and couldn't. As long as we keep Scarlett inside, she and our niece should be fine. But I think Thorpe might have answers we need. If he does, then Dylan can get them out of him, but we must get Zeke to make sure the pages they are looking for are still in the vault."

Colin moaned from behind him, the vampire sitting up and rubbing his jaw, his eyes darting up to Roman, who let the wolf bleed into his eyes, flashed his own sharp teeth, and snarled. "Run. Please run. Give me a chance to hunt you down. I will rip you apart, limb by limb. I will pull the flesh from your worthless body until you pass out, and then I'll wait until you wake up, until your skin has knitted back together, and then I will hunt you again, this time, gnawing on your bones while your screams play like music in my ears."

Colin Thorpe looked like he was about to be sick, and Roman snapped his teeth, nearly busting a gut when the weak-ass bitch fainted, the scent of his fear hitting Roman's nose.

Roman barely heard the screech of tires before he saw the car, shrouded in shadows with no headlights, only the scent of burning tires. Jasmine turned slightly, frowned, her eyes wide as if she were expecting the car to hit her. Realisation hit him like a punch; it was like she had seen this happening and she wasn't going to stop it.

Her eyes slid to his, and an emotion Roman could only describe as regret clouded her expression. She had this eerie calmness about her as she dropped her phone and turned to face the car that was aiming directly for her. She opened her mouth to speak as if she was frozen to the spot and unable to react, like she was shocked at this unexpected twist, when Roman knew that there was no way Jasmine hadn't seen this coming.

But Jasmine wasn't going to try and save herself.

Roman moved with preternatural speed, shoving Jasmine out of the way of the speeding car. The metal hitting his body, crushing his bones as the car threw him into the air and kept on driving, not even slowing. The pain overwhelmed him as he hit the tarmac hard. His head bounced off the ground, nausea rolling in his stomach, spots dancing in his vision as Jasmine's face came into view.

He heard her talking, that husky tone of hers that had given him devilish thoughts from the moment he had met her. He tried to get up, needed to move in case the car returned for another try, but his body wouldn't cooperate.

He heard his father's voice in his head calling him pathetic and weak. Mocking him for his inability to save yet another female. His mind started to sink to the past, darkness in his eyes even as Jasmine screamed his name, and then he was no longer in the present but shackled by his history.

Roman was surprised the house did not tremble under the weight of his father's rage, his fists beating down again on the table, the scent of his mother's fear ripe in the claustrophobic heat of the fire. Roman was cowered in the corner, his lanky frame no match for the alpha of their pack, even if he was his own father.

"The boy is defective. He cannot be mine. Cecile has given birth, and the toddler is already in fur. That screwup cannot be mine."

"I have never been unfaithful. Roman is your son."

His father turned to him, hate evident in his gaze. "I do not claim him as mine. You have failed to service your alpha and produce a worthy heir. I will take a new mate at the next full moon. It is a blessing, I suppose, that my wolf never accepted you as their true mate, lest I be shackled to you for eternity."

His mother sobbed, stepping closer to Roman and away from the male she had loved since they were both teens. Their match had been one of love, not how a wolf normally accepts a mate, but it had never bothered either of them until Roman was born.

His father grabbed his mother by the throat and lifted her off her feet. Roman growled and hurled himself at his father, hitting him as hard as he could, but it only made his father snicker as he swatted Roman with his free hand so hard that he felt his lip split.

"Since you are a whore who cannot keep her legs closed for other males, you will become less than the lowest wolf. Any wolf that wants to rut with you can, with my permission. And if you sire another defective pup, I will drown it before it reaches its second year of birth."

His mother was sobbing now as his father dragged her to the kitchen table, bent her over it, her head turned toward Roman, her eyes squeezed shut as his father freed himself from his pants, hiked up his mother's skirt, his hand pressing her neck to the table. Roman was powerless to do anything but watch as his father mounted his mother and she sobbed uncontrollably.

It was over in minutes.

His father withdrew, cast Roman a look, and then once he had zipped himself back inside his pants, his father flung the door open, revealing two of his pack members. The wolves lustfully looked at his mother, the evidence of their arousal in their scent and body.

Roman snarled and went to protect his mother, but his father grabbed him and held his body firmly. His mother begged his father to take Roman outside, that she would not resist if he didn't force her son to watch, but his father hadn't cared.

Roman nearly vomited when the first wolf raped his mother, struggling against his father's grasp, kicking and screaming even as his father told him to be quiet or he would be next.

Roman stomped on his father's foot, which distracted him long enough that Roman could then bolt for the door, ducking under his packmate's arm as he attempted to stop him. He ran and ran until his bare feet bled and until his sobs could be heard by no one but the wild animals in the forest around him.

He hid in a cave for weeks, using his penknife to hunt and kill rabbits, and used his skills to make a fire. He told himself that he would not return to the pack until he was bigger and stronger. Until he could be of use to his mother.

Perhaps his father would ease up on his mother by the time he came back.

"You are an abomination. A cancer within the pack. It is not natural for a shifter to be unable to change form. It is unacceptable for a wolf who carries the scent of a future alpha to be unable to fight as a wolf in a dominance battle. You are not my son. She must have rutted with some other degenerate behind my back."

Roman felt like an abomination. He had the wolf inside him, and it simply did not get to come out. Roman headed into the city and stayed at a shelter, his tallness meaning he could pass for older, and he ate his fill and then, a couple of months later, his body finally caught up with him, more bulk in his frame, more muscle on his bones.

He strode back into the pack site deep in the forest ready to free his mother from the shackles of his father, yet Roman was too late ... he had been too late and too weak to save her.

His mother's mind had become unravelled and completely undone. When the full moon called to her, she had shifted and had yet to come back. Now she hunted with the wild wolves; the wolves who had stayed in fur too long never returned.

He stood now, back in the forest, his father sneering and disgusted at his son, remarking how his other children, all female, had all been born with the ability to shift, and yet his father was cursed that his only son, a son who was an even stronger alpha than he was, could not become a wolf.

Roman stayed and fought to prove himself, challenge after challenge, until his father cast him from the pack rather than face his own son in a fight he would surely lose. Roman had killed all those who had laid a hand on his mother, who had defiled her and sent her to fur, where she would never be his mother again, lost to him forever.

Roman heard the sound of his name, felt the press of fingers to his lips, and he wanted to free himself from the memories, from the kid he used to be and the fact that he still felt immense guilt that he had not been able to save his mother, had been too late to save her.

"Come on, Roman. Stop lying down on the job. You stubborn fucking wolf. Open your fucking eyes. Dammit. Open your eyes."

And as the angelic voice demanded, Roman opened his eyes.

CHAPTER FIFTEEN

Jasmine

IT HAD FELT LIKE HER OWN BONES WERE SHATTERING THE MOMENT she saw the car ram right into Roman's body. Her scream lodged in her throat as he went up into the air in what seemed to be a slow-motion pace before his head hit the ground with a sickening thud. Then she had screamed his name, rushing forward, but Roman had lain motionless in the middle of the road.

Seconds later, Isolde had driven a team of Sicarius soldiers around the corner, securing Roman to a backboard and into the van. Isolde herself strode over to Colin and dragged him up by the collar, the vampire apparently having the sense not to anger the steely dragon any more than she already was.

Jasmine had jumped in the back with Roman, and when the team had attempted to take him to a medical unit, Jasmine had ordered them to take him to her own bedroom, which had raised a few eyebrows, and even Jasmine wasn't sure why she was so adamant that Roman be brought to her room.

Because you are falling for him. Because you are destined to fall for the wolf like no other, and it will either kill you or make you.

Doubt plagued her mind even now as the sun rose in the sky and Malakai, having come to check on them both, left to try and get some sleep for the day, but not before informing Jasmine that Colin was having some alone time with Dylan and Isolde.

That had made Jasmine smile. Her brother and Isolde had

the right skill set to interrogate their captive, and there was a reason why Dylan was one of the most sought-after interrogators in the human and Inferna world. His ability to sense emotions was invaluable.

Most prisoners just looked at Isolde and told her the truth instantly.

The medical team had stripped Roman of his clothes, so the wolf lay on her bed, arms by his side, dressed in just a pair of boxers. Jasmine had made Malakai sit with Roman while she changed in case he woke up and was alone. It was the fastest she had ever changed, and now she sat on the bed with her legs crossed, watching the rise and fall of Roman's chest.

When Malakai had asked her what happened, Jasmine could only tell him that Roman had saved her life, because she could not tell her brother that the reason why Roman was unconscious now was because she had seen the car approaching and something in her gut had told her that this was how she died. She had calculated the amount of blood needed to heal her body, and she wouldn't get enough in time. She had stood there ready to accept what would happen when Roman had pushed her out of the way, moving with a speed that seemed impossible, even for a wolf.

Jasmine couldn't resist the urge to touch him, to make sure that his heart was still beating. She trailed her fingers down his chest and lay her hand over his heart, relief sagging her at the steady *thump* that pulsed against her palm.

After Duke, Colin, whatever the hell his name was now, Jasmine wondered if it was just her touch that he didn't want. She'd wondered if something was wrong with her; had she been doing something wrong? But now she knew the wrongness in those thoughts when Roman kissed her, when he had curled up into her as they slept, how he had arched into her touch when she had cupped his erection.

Colin had taken away all the power she had as a woman,

and without even having sex with her, Roman had given it back.

"Come on, Roman. Stop lying down on the job. You stubborn fucking wolf. Open your fucking eyes. Dammit. Open your eyes."

Jasmine growled, lying back on the bed, and she sensed the change in Roman's breathing a second before Roman moved. He rolled on top of her, his eyes amber, his lips curled into a vicious snarl before they dropped to the curve of her neck, nipping at the flesh so hard that Jasmine let loose a hiss.

Roman lowered his body down on hers, and the hiss turned into a moan, her hands going through his tousled hair. When he nipped at her a little too hard, she scraped her nails along his scalp and said, "Too much, Roman."

That seemed to drag Roman back in control, his eyes bleeding from amber to brown instantly, Roman frowning as he took in his position and then hers. She saw the moment that he was going to pull back, so Jasmine linked her arms around his neck and pulled him down for a kiss.

She was the one to initiate the kiss, pressing her lips against his, once, twice, then she swept her tongue along his lips and it snapped the last of the control Roman had. He devoured her mouth, taking control of the kiss, and Jasmine let him. Each flick of his tongue, each nip on her lips, each clash of their teeth drove her insane as she arched her hips up, brushing against the hardness of Roman's cock that she wanted inside her.

Roman broke the kiss, his chest heaving, holding himself up on his elbows. "What are the chances one of your brothers is going to walk in on us?"

Jasmine chuckled, then spoke out loud. "Sicarius, initiate do not disturb mode on this floor. Alert me if anyone tries to bypass."

"Do not disturb mode initiated."

Roman shook his head as he grinned down at her. "That is genius. Your brother has one twisted mind."

Jasmine rolled her eyes, made to retort, but was silenced as Roman bent to kiss her throat, softer than the wolf had. Her body was on fire, a feat that should have been impossible for her kind, yet under Roman's touch, under the weight of his gaze, she felt like her soul was on fire for the very first time in her life.

She wanted. She needed. She craved.

Jasmine moved instinctively, rolling them so that she straddled him, her knees braced on either side of Roman's hips, his erection brushing against her already damp core. His big hands went to her hips, and she froze, her confidence gone as she chastised herself, knowing she was a fool for thinking a dominant like Roman would submit to her.

She began to scramble off Roman, but the wolf held her with an iron grip that made Jasmine think, just for a split second, that if Roman had not wanted her to roll them, then he could have stopped her.

"Hey, Jazz, what just went through your head?"

Jasmine shook her head, chewing on her bottom lip as Roman sat up, his stomach muscles flexing as he cupped her face, kissed her gently and then asked her again, "Tell me what ran through your head?"

He dropped his hands to the mattress but stayed sitting upright, his molten gaze holding hers. She was embarrassed to tell him that she was letting Colin into her head, especially now. But of course, Roman already knew, and he didn't recoil or chastise her. Instead, he kissed her briefly on the lips.

"Your ex has no hold over you, Jasmine, unless you let him. Any fantasies you have, I'm happy to let you indulge in them, and I am so on board for being ridden by you, you wouldn't believe it. I want to have your pretty mouth wrapped around my cock. I want you, Jasmine Cavanagh, all of you. Show me who you are."

Roman linked his hands behind his head, grinning up at her. Jasmine blinked, unsure of where to begin. She pulled off her tee, revealing her breasts, heat flooding her as Roman licked his lips. She hadn't bothered with a bra, so when she leaned in to kiss the curve of Roman's neck, her naked breasts rubbed against his chest, and they both groaned. She kissed her way down his chest, scraping her teeth over his nipples, encouraged by his sharp intake of breath.

Jasmine shifted so that she could trail her lips down lower and lower, slipping her hand inside the waistband of his boxers, wrapping her fingers around his cock, stroking once, twice, his skin like velvet in her grasp. The wolf closed his eyes and bit down hard enough on his bottom lip that a trickle of blood ran down his lips and chin.

Cock still in her grasp, she leaned up and licked the blood away. Roman barked out a curse that had Jasmine smiling. With her other hand, she freed Roman's cock, then shifted back so that she licked at the underside of the full length.

Roman was trembling under her touch, and she fucking loved it. His hands had now moved from behind his head to fist in the sheets, as if he was struggling to stop from reaching for her. She wanted him to lose control, to touch her without reservation, to come apart with her name on his lips, just as she had when he had expertly used that mouth of his on her core, his tongue licking her until she could not think.

Before she could talk herself out of it, Jasmine scooted farther down the bed, lowered her head and guided the head of Roman's cock into her mouth. His growl vibrated along his body, straight to his cock, adding another sensation to the erotic feeling of having this strong, dominant man at her mercy.

She wasn't as skilled at this as she would have liked, but the way Roman's hardness twitched in her mouth, she knew she wasn't doing too badly. She took more of him inside her mouth, then repeated it, unable to get all of him inside her.

She hollowed her cheeks, let her fangs elongate and then gently trail along his flesh as she sucked.

She flicked her tongue over the head, tasted the essence of her wolf, and then she was pulled off his cock, her back on the bed, her shorts and panties tossed over Roman's shoulder. He stripped off his own boxers and stood at the foot of her bed, gloriously naked, fisting his own cock.

"I wanted to make you come with my mouth," Jasmine teased him as Roman growled. She laughed, feeling as if her heart was beating and full.

"Later. Now I need to be inside you or my cock is gonna break in two."

"Can't have that now, can we, wolf. Come have your wicked way with me."

And yet Roman didn't move, just worked his cock with a glint of mischief in his eyes. "Are you ready for me, darling? Let me see you dip a finger inside yourself and check for me."

She realized then that Roman was playing with her, teasing her and tempting her, and making this as fun as possible. He was showing her that her wants and her needs were nothing more than something a normal couple shared in the bedroom.

She slid her hand slowly down her stomach, Roman's eyes following the path it travelled, and when she dipped a single finger into her core, she nearly came apart watching the hunger flare in his eyes. She moved her finger in and out, mimicking the movements Roman's cock would make, adding a second finger as she groaned and her head fell back.

Jasmine hadn't felt Roman move, hadn't noticed the dip in the mattress, but suddenly his hands were on her wrist, pulling her fingers out and into his own mouth. He sucked on her fingers with as much effort as she had his cock, and she jerked her hips up.

"Now, Roman. I need to feel you inside me now." Her tone was heady, breathless even, which she considered was ridiculous since she didn't *need* to breathe. But Roman made her feel things she thought were long dead.

She felt Roman's hands on her thighs, felt her legs spread open, anticipation in her veins, as Roman positioned himself at her entrance. And still the wolf didn't penetrate her.

"I think the next time, I'm gonna let you ride me, Jazz. I want to see you bouncing up and down on my cock, your breasts falling against you, your head thrown back. I like the idea of being taken by you. Then I'm going to kiss and touch every inch of you until you beg me to take you, and only then, when you ask me ever so nicely, am I going to give you my cock.

"I'm gonna take you back to the cabin so that your scent is on my sheets," Roman continued as Jasmine felt herself nearing the edge of reason at his words. "I want to chase you through the forest and catch you, then fuck you in the grass. I want to learn how to make you gasp, what makes you moan, what gets you as wet as you are now. But now, now I want you to dig your nails and your teeth into my skin."

Jasmine made to retort, but then Roman had the head of his erection at her entrance. He rotated his hips, pushing into her slowly. Jasmine gripping his shoulders, her walls stretched at his size. Roman dropped his head to kiss her slowly, then he inched in a little more every time he slid in and out, the feel of him like a brand inside her, as if this, as if he was something she would not recover from.

Jasmine felt her orgasm building, needed all of him in her right now as the wolf moved torturously slow. She bit down hard on his shoulder, hoping to snap his control, earning a chortle of laughter from the wolf, and it dawned on her that the only one close to losing control was her.

Hooking her legs around his, Jasmine tried to pull him in closer, but the wolf resisted her challenge. Roman continued to make love to her slowly, her orgasm building and building, and as he stroked in and out of her, sometimes pulling out completely before he pushed his way into her again, Jasmine thought she was going to lose her mind.

The muscles in Roman's neck stretched, and Jasmine knew then he was close to loosening the reins on his control. Jasmine waited until Roman lowered his head, then she struck, sinking her fangs into his throat, swallowing hard, and that snapped the last of Roman's control.

With a growl that raised every hair on her body, Roman pulled out of her, bent her knee back, and then he entered her completely in one single movement, and Jasmine came. Roman moved at a much harder pace, pounding into her, the metal on the canopy shaking under the way he drove into her, Jasmine having just ridden the wave off one orgasm when another threatened to hit.

On the brink of madness, Jasmine sucked on his throat. The swallow of his blood made her yank her fangs from his flesh and cry out his name as she trembled, her mind splintering as Roman gave one final thrust and moaned her name as he came, holding himself inside her as he emptied his seed into her. He lowered himself to kiss her throat, and she laughed as she felt his cock twitch inside her as she licked closed the wound at this throat.

They lay in a tangle of limbs, not uttering a word for a few minutes, until Roman rolled them, pulling out of her so that she could lay sprawled on top of him. His chest was rising quickly after the exertion. He pressed his lips to the top of her head, and Jasmine felt like the princess in all of those romcoms she loved so much who had finally found the other half of her soul.

Roman rested his palm on the curve of her ass as Jasmine wondered if the thrill of the chase would wear off now Roman had gotten what he wanted. Would he back off, or would she?

Pain laced her head as she scrambled into a seated position, and she felt her eyes glaze over.

"Rivers of blood to create an endless night. Blood of the innocent to reveal his plans. She will come to break his heart, and it will start the beginning of the end. Death can still be defeated. The mother can still lose. The truth must be revealed in order to prevent the past from taking hold. He comes. He comes."

Jasmine came back to herself with a gasp, this vision being clearer than she had seen in a long time. Not since she'd had the vision of Dante's death and she had ignored it. She had seen Keeva's death at the hands of the villain they chased. Had seen Scarlett's death at the loss of her child because sometimes a person could be living but be dead of emotion. She knew she had to tell her brothers the truth about Dante's death, but she didn't know where to start.

She felt Roman's hand on the base of her spine, rubbing comforting circles as she glanced over her shoulder at him. Jasmine wanted to curl up and sleep the day away beside him before reality came back to haunt them, before they had to leave for the cabin and the clock that ticked down the hours to when she could return home and face all her brothers and tell them exactly what had happened.

With a wicked grin, Jasmine edged off the bed, backing away as she crooked her fingers at Roman. "We made a mess. I think we need to wash up." Jasmine ducked her eyes downward, smiling when she saw that Roman's cock was already hardening. "Unless you aren't up to it, wolf?"

Roman's growl was all she needed to know that he was down for a shower cleanup, and she shrieked with glee as he darted off the bed and stalked toward her. She was putty in his touch as he dropped to his knees in the shower even before she managed to turn on the water.

CHAPTER SIXTEEN

Roman

ROMAN WAS NOT A RELIGIOUS MAN, YET HE FELT THAT IF THERE was a heaven, then it would feel just as good as it did to have Jasmine in his arms. They had left the Sicarius compound just after dark and had been naked since they crossed the threshold of the cabin.

Jasmine had been quiet as they drove, but the moment Roman pulled to a stop outside the cabin, she took off her seat belt and crawled into his lap. It had been a hard, furious fuck that had squeezed his balls and had him coming in minutes.

Now they lay sprawled on the rug in front of the fire, Jasmine half on, half off his body, her fingers tapping in time with the beat of his heart. They hadn't discussed her apparent failure to react when the car was hurtling toward her or that he had taken serious damage by taking the hit meant for her.

"Do you still wish you could shift?"

Her question came suddenly, breaking through the silence as Roman pulled her closer to him. "I used to. I spent a lot of time and money searching for a cure, as if there was something wrong with me. Yet in the end, all it took was getting to meet Conor, who accepted me despite the fact I could not be like him, to know that there was nothing wrong with me."

"I could, yano …" she began, shifting so that she hovered over him, her blue eyes filled with determination. "I could try what I did with Scarlett, see if I could, I dunno?"

As Jasmine shrugged, Roman pulled her down for a kiss.

"Thank you. I'm good. I don't see it as a weakness, Jazz. More of an extra weapon in my arsenal. But I appreciate that you want to try and fix me."

Jasmine's frown deepened, and then she punched him hard in the shoulder.

"Hey!" Roman exclaimed. "What was that for?"

"You don't need to be fixed, Roman. I just wanted to see if whatever mojo I have could help."

Roman's heart stuttered, and he made to answer her back when he heard a horn blare outside, then a voice shouted, "Roman!"

Roman growled and thumped his head against the floorboards. "Conor always had piss-poor timing."

Jasmine laughed as she got to her feet, holding out her hand to help him up. "Better go shower and make myself presentable."

"We could save water? Shower together," Roman teased with a grin, filled with pride as Jasmine rolled her eyes.

"Puh-lease. If we get in the shower together, it will be morning before you go out to Conor and Abbie. Separate showers, mister."

Roman was laughing as he pulled a throw around his waist and went to the door. He spotted Conor lounging on the bonnet of his car, Abbie resting her hip against the side. The scent that wafted through the air made Roman's stomach rumble, and he grinned at his friends.

"You know where everything is. Least you can do for showing up unannounced is get it set up."

Roman showered and dressed quickly, throwing on shorts and a tee, then headed out into the kitchen area, where Abbie was scooping ice out of the freezer and into a cool box. Roman went to help her, taking some beer out of the fridge, taking the box, and carrying it outside for her, earning a raised brow in return.

"You do remember I'm a wolf too, right?"

Roman only chuckled, striding outside to where Conor and Jasmine were setting plates and cutlery on the table. Jasmine had pulled her hair back into a slick ponytail and dressed in a tank top and shorts that said *Juicy* on the butt. She smiled over at Roman, and damn if he didn't melt a little.

"You love her!"

It wasn't a question but a statement in Abbie's whispered tone. Did he love Jasmine? He had never felt like this about another person in his life. He wanted her with him at all times. He loved the sensations that raced in his veins when he made her laugh. He dreaded the thought of her going back to normal once her self-imposed exile was done.

The wolf told him time and time again that Jasmine was his mate.

And Roman finally admitted to himself that he fucking hoped like hell it was the truth.

He wasn't going to say to Abbie exactly how he felt when he wanted Jasmine to be the first to know it. He glanced at Abbie, who just smiled and patted him on the arm. "It's okay. I already know the answer because you look at her the way my Conor looks at me."

Conor waved them over, and Roman held out his arm to escort Abbie to the table, pulling out the chair beside Conor like the gentleman he was. Conor did the same for Jasmine, so as not to be outdone. Abbie shook her head, glancing at Jasmine.

"Those two are always trying to outdo the other. They once ended up with food poisoning because they had a bet going that they could eat a whole trough of this mystery meat that the staff had cooked up when we were in Afghanistan. They ate until they physically couldn't eat anymore, and then they were out of commission for like three days. You'll get used to it."

"I get it. My brother, Dylan, they call us twins because we look so alike, but he is older than me. We always have friendly competitions with each other. Neither of us likes to lose. Thankfully Malakai has a cool head and stops us before we go too far."

"By Jaysus, not another one."

They all laughed, then tucked into the food. Roman didn't realize how starving he really was until he had devoured a whole plate of fried chicken. He washed it down with a little beer, and the night passed with an ease that made Roman deliriously happy.

Conor jumped out of his seat, pulling the axes Roman used to chop wood. He had a smile as big as Texas as he rushed to pull the targets out of storage, Roman got up and helped him set them up. They then proceeded to toss the axes at the targets like they had done whenever they were deployed, and then also when they were home, insisting they only did it to sharpen their skills.

Roman was surprised when Jasmine got to her feet, holding out her hand for an axe. Conor gave her one, then started to tell her how to throw it, taking a couple more axes and asking Jasmine to hit certain parts of the board.

Roman was not in the least bit surprised that Jasmine hit every target without even a flinch. However, Conor's jaw dropped to the floor as Jasmine flicked her hair off her shoulder.

"How the hell can you throw so good?"

Jasmine patted his best friend on the cheek. "I have Norse blood in me. We came here as children, and I was trained to fight by Vikings and shieldmaidens. It would be a dishonour to the gods if I couldn't throw an axe."

As Jasmine strode over to collect the axes, Conor flashed him a toothy grin, a thumbs-up, and then he mouthed, "If you don't marry this woman, I will use an axe to cut off your balls."

Competition over, Conor and Abbie told them that they had made Hiro and Ezra fix the windows and any other damage and left them in charge. They told Roman they were planning on hitting the road and taking a vacation.

Abbie mentioned that they had planned to head on a trip for Christmas but the team had shown up just before they were meant to leave, and so they had stayed and spent Christmas with them instead.

Jasmine let out a frustrated breath, causing them all to look at her.

"Oh, don't mind me," she said with a wave of her hand. "I missed all the best holidays while I was … unwell. I love Halloween and Christmas and New Year's. Even Valentine's Day. Me and Dylan go all out with the party planning, and I even had the best dress ever for New Year's that made me look like a disco ball! Guess I'll have to wait now until next year. Well, at least Paddy's Day is around the corner."

Jasmine sipped her beer, then looked wistfully out at the water, only Roman seeing the sadness in her eyes.

"They want us to come in next month and interview for a role with Sicarius." Conor glanced at Jasmine before he continued. "Everyone but Ezra got a call, but I suspect that's to do with how he knew your Jasmine before."

If Jasmine didn't like being called his, she didn't show it. She just shrugged. "I just show up to interviews when asked, and it's not like they take my advice on anything. I was blatantly clear that Roman was a no and still, here he is."

Her tone was light, her eyes dancing as she winked at him. Conor laughing as Abbie shook her head.

"Who called you?" Jasmine asked, taking a drink from her beer bottle.

"It was a Ms. Russell. She asked us to come next month."

"Ah, then Malakai himself will do the interview. He must value Roman's word if he is doing that himself." Jasmine drank her beer, and then she turned her head, looking out into the forest. Her body tensed, and she dropped the beer bottle, the glass smashing to the ground at Jasmine's bare feet.

"The forest has claws and teeth to claim you. Scars and blood and bone. Beware the traitor in your midst. It is those you least expect who will stab you in the front."

Jasmine made to get up, embarrassment in her scent, afraid of what Conor and Abbie would think, and Roman was up out of his chair to stop her from walking on broken glass. But Conor got there before him.

He dropped to a knee in front of Jasmine, one hand on her ankle as he plucked the glass off the ground and set it on the table. Abbie got up and started clearing the table as Roman stayed where he was, watching Conor look after Jasmine.

"It's all right, Jasmine. Your secrets will not be spilled by any of us. We would take your secrets to the grave."

"Well, hopefully that won't happen anytime soon," she drawled out sarcastically, pulling a hoot of laughter from Conor.

He let go of her ankle, sweeping a hand along the ground to check for more glass.

"All clear."

Conor went to stand, stopping in a crouch as Jasmine reached out and cupped his cheek. Roman leaned forward and saw her eyes go white, and then they were blue again.

"Take Abbie to Paris. Enjoy the alone time. I'll tell Malakai to keep Abbie in mind for an ops role for the moment."

"I don't understand," Conor stuttered as he looked from Jasmine to Roman, then back at the vampire.

Jasmine shrugged. "She can't go on active missions in her condition."

Anger flared in Conor's eyes, hurt as he turned his head to Roman, as if he had betrayed their friendship by spilling secrets that were not his. Jasmine, sensing the discord, placed a hand on the side of Conor's face, drawing it back to hers.

"You have lost, and you both have mourned. I would never lie about something like this. Go to Paris. Let her tell you. The fates told me that I needed you to know this, but let her tell you herself."

Conor's anger washed away from his face, fear now in his eyes. "What if we can't hold on to this one too?"

"That is not your path. Your babies are meant for more."

Conor sat back in the grass in disbelief. "Babies? As in more than one?"

Jasmine offered him a brilliant smile and tapped her nose. "I will let that be a surprise. Sorry if I spoiled it, but when I am urged to tell someone something, I cannot avoid it."

Conor was still sitting in the grass when Abbie came outside and took one look at her husband and asked him what was wrong. Conor had yet to gather himself, so Jasmine turned round in her chair and grinned at Abbie.

"I don't think your husband likes me much anymore. He just found out that I support Manchester United."

"Blasphemy, that is, Abbie darling. I no longer condone their relationship."

Abbie eyed them all suspiciously but accepted their response as Conor got off the ground and went to kiss his wife. She swatted him away, and they all sat down again until Jasmine yawned loudly, then covered her mouth.

"I'm sorry. But the sun will rise soon. I'll say goodbye now and see you all soon."

Jasmine waved cheerily, then vanished into the house as the first rays of the sun broke through the cloud and Conor got to his feet. "We didn't mean to stay all night."

Roman clapped him on the back. "It's all good. It was nice to have company. It reminded me that this is only a temporary bubble we are in. Normality will come back to us if we let it."

Abbie pulled him down to kiss his cheek, then patted his chest, before leaving him and Conor alone. They walked a little away from both the cabin and the car, hopefully out of earshot, before Conor folded his arms across his chest and leaned against a tree.

"She's your mate."

"Ya, she is."

"Does she know it?" Conor asked.

"No," Roman answered with a sigh. "She was hurt, before me, and I don't want to rattle her. She hated shifters when we met, and I have no idea why. I can't tell her that she is it for me until she is certain that I am it for her."

"You seem at ease when you are with her. That burden you carry doesn't look as heavy. I want you to be as happy as I am with my Abbie. Don't let her issues or, hell, my brother, your issues sink into your bones with claws that won't come out. Show her where you came from, and maybe she will show you who she is."

Roman was still standing where Conor left him half an hour later, unsure of what to do next. He ran his hands through his hair, giving himself a few minutes to think, before it dawned on him.

"I missed all the best holidays while I was … unwell. I love Halloween and Christmas, and New Year's. Even Valentine's Day. Me and Dylan go all out with the party planning, and I even had the best dress ever for New Year's that made me look like a disco ball! Guess I'll have to wait now until next year."

Pulling out his phone, Roman placed a call and called in every favour he had to his name from his colleagues. When he called Keeva, the banshee answered with a grumpy curse, but when he explained what he wanted to do, she chuckled down the phone and told him that he was fighting dirty.

"You ain't seen nothing yet."

He hung up after another half hour of making calls and then headed back to the cabin. He went right into the bedroom, pausing in the doorway, and watching Jasmine as she scrolled through her phone. She looked up at him, and damn, she was utterly captivating.

"I had fun tonight," she said as she set down her phone.

"I want to take you on a proper date."

Jasmine lowered her lashes, kept her eyes closed for an agonising heartbeat before she opened them again and, with that haughty tone of hers, remarked, "You already have me in your bed, Roman. No need to try and romance me now."

Roman wanted to tell her that he wanted to take her to dinner so she could see that he wanted more than just sex with her. He wanted to walk in public with her and let every son of a bitch who ran their eyes over her know that she was his. She had chosen him. He wanted her to see that they could be more than physical because they obviously had that down to a fine art.

But he kept all of that to himself as he said, "Humour me, okay? Maybe I'm a hopeless romantic at heart, or maybe I'm sick of cooking and would like a proper steak. So, dinner? You and me? Out in public like grown-ups? We can keep it casual."

She eyed him suspiciously for a minute, then she grinned. "I think you need to convince me, wolf."

She threw back the covers to reveal her glorious naked body, and Roman's mouth went dry. She palmed one of her breasts, pulling her lower lip between her teeth. Her other hand snaked down her body, between her legs, like she knew Roman liked watching her touch herself. She kept her eyes on him as she pushed a finger inside her and groaned.

"Oh, that feels good," she breathed huskily, then her eyes went devilish as she stated, "But not as good as when your cock is in me. I want to feel you push into me, feel the burn as my walls milk your cock and then you take me hard and fast until all I can think is your name and nothing else."

Roman was already taking off his tee when she flicked her nipples and called his name in a tone that had him rock-hard in seconds. She was still pleasuring herself as he divested himself of his shorts and boxers, and then he did as his mate asked, took her hard and fast until she screamed his name and scored his back with her nails.

He was relentless in his pursuit to win her over, driving into her until his balls drew up and he came with a grunt, thrusting into her over and over as he emptied himself into her, Jasmine clenching around his cock as she came again.

It was only when he had taken her twice more, and his vampire was all drowsy and well-loved, did Jasmine agree to go on a date with him.

CHAPTER SEVENTEEN

Jasmine

JASMINE WAS A KNOT OF ANXIETY.

When they had woken this morning, Roman told her to dress super casual, that tonight was all about fun. She dressed in leggings that were stretchy in case someone tried to ruin their night again and a loose T-shirt that had "badass" across the chest. She slipped on a short hoodie and tied her hair back into a high ponytail, and Jasmine slipped her feet into a pair of pink Nikes before stepping outside.

Roman was crouched down lacing up his boots, dressed in well-worn jeans, a khaki-coloured tee, and a camo shirt thrown on over it. He glanced up when she entered the room, getting to his feet with a grin.

"You ready?" Roman asked, his eyes dancing, brightening his entire face.

Jasmine nodded, unable to disperse the sense of foreboding, as if she knew something bad was coming but the fates had decided not to bother warning her about it. She let herself be led to the car, Roman's hand on the small of her back.

She didn't speak until they were on the main road, having received a message from Dylan.

"Colin hasn't done much talking, according to Dylan. Looks like he was trying to find a new way to power by siding with the enemy."

"Spineless prick," Roman growled, his grip tightening on

the steering wheel, and Jasmine decided it was best not to ruin the evening by talking about douchebag exes.

Roman drove through Midleton, out to what looked like a football pitch, but Jasmine saw an array of lights and heard music before she saw the big wheel, the roller coaster, and felt her chest expand as Roman pulled into a spot.

"Oh my god ... our date is at a fairground?"

The wolf offered her a sly curve of his lips. "Should be fun."

Roman jumped out of the car, walked around and opened her door for her, then held out his hand for her to take. She slipped her hand into his, surprised at how natural it felt and a little terrified. Roman locked the car, then headed for the entrance, where he skipped the queue, nodding to the teen at the gate before escorting Jasmine inside.

Jasmine loved the fanfare of it, forgetting her trepidations and letting herself be led around the fairground that ran around in a circle. Humans and Inferna milled about the areas, with children darting in and out of stalls as their parents chased after them.

Roman kept his hand in hers as he turned and walked backwards. "So, what do you want to do first?"

Jasmine had little fear when it came to stuff like this. She and Dylan had gone and done every extreme thing you could think of. She pulled Roman to the bumper cars, resulting in a hilarious incident where Roman got in the way of any man, woman, or child who tried to bump Jasmine. She laughed heartily at Roman's attempts at chivalry, then proceeded to recruit the kids to gang up on Roman, and the poor wolf couldn't move without getting hit.

Jasmine made him go on every ride, then whipped out her phone and took a selfie to post later once they were home because she didn't want to alert anyone to her whereabouts and do anything to spoil the merriment. Roman slung his arm around her shoulders, the heat of him against her a calming influence, and she could almost ignore the sense of dread forming in the pit of her stomach.

Roman detangled himself from her to stride forward to a shooting game, winking over his shoulder as he dug into his pocket, paid, and proceeded to hit every target spot-on, much to the vendor's chagrin. He frowned as Roman nailed each shot and then accused him of cheating.

She expected Roman to lose his temper, but the wolf just laughed and told the vendor that he had been in the army for years and his sergeant would have busted his balls if he missed an easy shot like that. The two then fell into old war stories as Jasmine glanced around and waited patiently.

Roman beckoned her over and asked her what prize she wanted. Jasmine let her gaze roam over the stuffed animals, and her smile widened as she pointed.

"I want the pineapple."

"The pineapple? Really?" Roman asked with a bemused expression that Jasmine thought bordered on cute.

"Yup. The pineapple."

The vendor was shaking his head, telling Roman his girl was a little weird, and when Roman offered Jasmine a dazzling smile that heated her blood and made her stomach flutter, it was as if he wanted to tell her he knew.

Roman handed her the pineapple, which looked just like a normal pineapple but squishy, and she crooked her finger to Roman, who ducked his head so Jasmine could give him a peck on the lips. Then she linked her arm in his as they headed to the food area.

Jasmine snagged a table, which was a picnic bench set up in a little section with food trucks all around. Roman queued for maybe ten minutes before he returned with greasy burgers, fries, and ice-cold Cokes. They ate in relative silence, their shoulders touching, Roman giving Jasmine a weird look when she dipped her fries into her Coke and then did the same and held a dripping fry out to Roman.

The wolf bit into it, his face contorting into a grimace before he swallowed.

"That's disgusting."

Considering that Roman looked like he was going to vomit, she would take his word for it, but she still dipped another fry in and ate it as Roman rolled his eyes. She leaned into his shoulder, felt his hand go around her back and rest on the seat behind her, and she let loose a contented sigh.

A kite landed on their table, and Roman reached out to take it in his grasp, then stood, glancing around to see who it might belong to. A little boy about six or seven ran toward Roman, his cheeky grin as wide as he was tall, his eyes widening at Roman's height, so the wolf went down into a crouch to hand the little kid back his kite.

Jasmine saw the moment that Roman tensed and Jasmine braced herself for an attack, yet Roman was focused on the wolf that had arrived into the food area, so Jasmine studied him.

The wolf had brown hair shaved close to the head with blue eyes that seemed murky. There was a faint scar from his lip to his chin that made his face look severe, and he was short in stature. Jasmine knew he was a wolf because of his scent, then she noticed that the boy had the same kind of scent as the other wolf ... and so did Roman.

Roman ruffled the kid's hair before rising to his full height as the other man sent the boy, Rocco, to go find his mother, leaving Roman and the wolf staring at each other. Jasmine saw Roman clench and unclench his fists as the man spoke.

"You look well."

"Since when do you give a fuck how I look?"

The man sighed, like Roman's reluctance to be polite inconvenienced him. "I see your time with vampires has not improved your manners. Really, son, after thirty years, do you not wish to let the past go?"

Roman flinched like his father had hit him, a growl in his

throat as he replied, "Have you seen my mother lately? Or have you been too busy trying to secure an heir that you forget what you did to your first wife?"

"I heard you were working for the Primus now at his security company. Hired muscle? You never were really any good at much else, and they certainly can't have hired you for your brains. I'm surprised they even wanted you at all in the first place."

The other wolf, Roman's father, slid his gaze to Jasmine, and she instantly felt grubby.

"Does she know what you are? Does she understand your *defects?*" The wolf inhaled and then laughed. "Of course, I suspect it is better to rut a corpse than it is a living creature considering you wouldn't want to reproduce more defective wolves."

Jasmine was on her feet and standing between the two wolves a second later. "Now, now. There are humans here, and we need to be careful." She felt Roman's growl against the palm of her hand as she placed it on his chest before she gave Roman's father a sly grin. "Not that I wouldn't like to see Roman hand you your ass, but I'd hate to embarrass you in front of your kid."

Jasmine inclined her head, and the other wolf looked back to where the small boy stood. Roman's father spat on the ground right by his oldest son's feet and then pivoted to clutch the little boy's hand and drag him away. Jasmine had hoped that the idiot's departure would lessen the tension in Roman, but he stalked to the table, grabbed his half-eaten food and dumped it in the bin before storming away, leaving Jasmine to follow after him.

Guess date night was over …

Roman was already in the car as Jasmine got in, her pineapple in her lap. Roman peeled out of the car park and onto the road. Jasmine gave him a few minutes, then decided to broach the subject.

"Want to tell me what happened back there?"

"No." A one-word answer was not a good start.

"Okay, but maybe if you talk to me about it, it might help."

"Do you tell me all your fucking secrets?" Roman sounded vicious, like he was seconds away from losing his control and punching the dashboard.

"Please don't make this about me," she said quietly as Roman laughed.

"Isn't it always about you, Jasmine?"

Jasmine clamped her mouth shut, hugged her pineapple to her, and turned her head to gaze out the window. Maybe it was a good thing that she was going home tomorrow. They had essentially gone from zero to sixty in their relationship, and maybe, after Roman's encounter, they needed a little space.

She had always assumed that Roman's parents were dead because he never spoke of them, yet they were both alive and well by the sounds of it. How much about the real Roman did she know? He knew nearly everything about her life, knew her brothers, knew about her powers, and while Roman had introduced her to his friends, she still felt like she barely knew him.

Or was she just picking at threads to unravel her feelings?

The car stopped just outside the cabin, and Roman had the ignition off and was out in the forest before Jasmine had even taken off her seat belt. She set the pineapple down in the car because she sure as hell wasn't about to have a conversation with him while she was holding a pineapple in the middle of his forest.

"What are we doing here, Jasmine? Where are we going with us?"

Jasmine wasn't expecting those sorts of questions, even if she had been contemplating them herself. She wasn't sure what tomorrow would bring, for them at least, but after the last week, they couldn't go back to the way they were before.

Did she want Roman to come and be with her at Sicarius? To spend her life with him? Was he her soul mate like Keeva and Scarlett had been for her brothers, or was it going to be Roman that killed her in the end?

Jasmine didn't want to die but knew if it was the path chosen for her, then she was just an unwilling participant in the destination. She walked to where Roman stood, placed her hands on his stomach, and felt his muscles tense at her touch.

"I need to know what you want from me, Jasmine."

His tone was even, deadly calm, and Jasmine didn't like how he sounded.

Jasmine felt panic rise in her chest and did her best to try and get Roman to think about other, more distracting things. She trailed her hand up his chest, a wicked grin curving her lips up as she popped the first button of Roman's shirt.

"I don't want to waste time talking. Tomorrow, I go back to Sicarius and Dante's. Normality sucks."

Roman growled and grabbed her wrists, gentler than his darkened expression portrayed. "So, what? You want one more fuck from the wolf before you have to go back to pretending that I disgust you? Don't want any of your so-called friends, ones who haven't bothered to contact you since you woke up, knowing that you liked a bit of rough with the hired help, right?"

Jasmine snatched her wrists away. "That's not what I meant at all."

"No?" Roman snarled, his face reddening with anger. "Then what the hell did you mean?"

She knew that Roman had been rattled this evening, that whatever was in his past had led to him getting this angry with her because of it. That anger had been rooted in how

Roman was really feeling, that he wanted answers that Jasmine wasn't sure she could give right now.

Jasmine's head was spinning, reeling from the suddenness of Roman's change of attitude, wondering if it had anything to do with the family of wolves they had interacted with at the fairground. They had been having such a nice time, and then, boom, it was like Roman had morphed into a different person, an angry person.

But the problem was, she didn't know what she wanted.

"The prophetess will lose herself to a wolf like no other. It will either be her end or her awakening."

The fucking curse or prophecy or whatever the hell it was had begun to seriously mess with her head. She didn't trust how she was feeling, what she was feeling, and she was so confused. What parts of her feelings were destinies attempting to play tricks with her and what was she actually feeling?

Sometimes, the truth doesn't always set you free.

"I'm not sure," she admitted, taking a step closer to Roman, hoping the proximity would lessen this heated discussion.

Roman gently pushed her away and took a step back, putting a vastness between them that make Jasmine's chest ache. "I wasn't planning on keeping whatever this is between us a secret. I'm not that guy. I don't want to be shady. I want everyone to know that this is something. But I guess I've been reading this all wrong, eh?"

"I ... we ... um ... why do we have to complicate things?" The moment the words tumbled from her mouth, Jasmine instantly felt stupid, like she couldn't stop the verbal diarrhoea flowing out of her mouth, making this situation completely worse.

Roman barked out a bitter-sounding laugh. "Complicate things? Pretending we haven't spent the last few days naked complicates things. I wanted to punch that dickhead ex of yours in the face, and that was before we complicated things." He spat the word *complicated* like it was a curse. "So what? You expect me to stand by, watch as you flirt with other men, and rein in my wolf so I don't break some asshole's face because he dared put his hands on you?"

Jasmine stepped back, feeling as if Roman had scalded her, his brown eyes filled with such an intensity, such hurt, and all she could do was stare at him like she didn't understand the words he spoke to her.

"Can we not just keep this between us?" Jasmine asked in a quiet voice she did not even recognise herself.

"Hell no," Roman snarled, his voice more wolf than man. "I never thought you were that kinda woman, the one who was ashamed to let people know that she has gotten down and dirty with the bodyguard. Do you think I'm less than you are? The Jasmine I have spent the last week with wouldn't have cared about what other people thought of her. They wouldn't have cared who she was with. This Jasmine, this persona for the masses, I don't want to know her at all."

His words hurt her more than Jasmine could have ever imagined, sparking her own fear and anger. She swept her hair off her shoulders. "And what? You thought this was serious? Like we were headed for blissful normalcy like Malakai and Keeva? Puh-lease. It was fun, but you and me, it was never gonna be long term, was it?"

The anger bled from Roman's face, and all she saw was bitter disappointment. He looked defeated, as if he knew she would, or could, never want to be with him. She saw it the moment Roman understood and accepted it.

"The cabin's yours for the day. I'll text Dylan the coordinates and the security stuff. He can collect you tomorrow after sunset, and then we never have to cross paths again. Goodbye, Jasmine."

His words seemed so final, like a door slamming in her face as Roman stalked into the forest, vanishing into the night like a wraith. Jasmine just stood there, wishing she could take it all back, to tell Roman she didn't mean what she had said and that it was only because she was terrified that she was falling in love with him.

Tears cascaded down her face, even as she ducked inside the cabin to hide from the sun, and she was still crying as she stood in the doorway of the cabin, bags packed, as Dylan drove up beside Roman's car. She sobbed when Dylan jumped out of the car, took one look at her face, and engulfed her in a hug.

"Aw, Jazz, you're in love with him."

Jasmine cried into her brother's shoulder, hugging him closely, unable to say the words that she wanted to say aloud, in case Roman heard them from where he hid in the forest and it undid all the damage she had done with her words.

She had fallen for Roman Lowe, and the prophecy had been dead on.

It was her undoing.

CHAPTER EIGHTEEN

Jasmine

J ASMINE COULDN'T SLEEP, HADN'T BEEN ABLE TO SLEEP ALL DAY as she adjusted to lying in a bed alone again. Her conversation with Roman went round and round in her head. She had been so worried about the prophecy, about what it might mean, that she had hurt the man who had done nothing but let her be who she was. Roman had allowed her to shine, and she had slapped him in the face for it.

She wasn't ashamed to say she missed him. Not just the amazing sex but his company. Roman was an easy listener, always ready with a smile and a snappy comeback. There was no falseness with the wolf, and Jasmine loved that about him.

Picking up her phone for the millionth time, Jasmine sighed when she saw no messages, tapped at her phone, and made to press call on the screen as she chewed on her lip and then tossed the phone aside.

Pain stabbed at her forehead, and Jasmine hissed, pressing her palms to her forehead before the vision took her.

"I need to talk to you, Kai. You and Dylan and Zeke."

Malakai turned away from Keeva to look at her, concern in his always watchful eyes. Something in her face must have spooked him because his gaze narrowed, and he pulled out his phone.

"I'll go," Keeva said, but Jasmine held up her hand.

"Kai will only tell you after. You might as well stay."

Jasmine sat at the kitchen table, her eyes looking out to the night as she finally was ready to confess her sins to her brothers, and she feared they would cast her out. She deserved it, she did. Especially with how she had lied to them for centuries.

It would destroy her to lose them.

The pain dulled as Jasmine blinked to clear her vision, glancing at her phone to see an hour had passed and the sun had barely dipped behind the horizon. She sprang from the bed, threw on a hoodie over her pyjamas, and headed upstairs, where she knew her eldest brother would be.

The elevator opened into the family area, and Jasmine stepped inside, taking a moment to watch the easy interaction between Malakai and Keeva. Keeva sat perched on the break-fast bar, dressed in shorts and one of Malakai's T-shirts, her tangle of red curls loose as she laughed at something Malakai said, hitting him on the shoulder with a wooden spoon. Malakai pretended to growl, a slow smile curving his lips as he took a step toward his fiancé and then stopped to look up at Jasmine.

Malakai had to have known she was there—the elevator was loud enough—but Jasmine wanted to leave them to their slice of happiness. Everyone within the Inferna and human communities had been completely surprised when millionaire bachelor Malakai had fallen for a relative nobody. But Keeva had been so much more than that, a woman who had not thrown herself at Kai, had a will so strong and a loyalty to those she loved, it was easy to see why Malakai had been drawn to her.

"Jasmine."

Malakai said her name, and it snapped her out of her thoughts. For a hot minute, Jasmine considered not acting on the vision, keeping her secret to herself, and not losing all that she loved. Panic welled in her chest as the pain in her head intensified, as if she was being told that not telling her brothers the truth was not an option.

"I need to talk to you, Kai. You and Dylan and Zeke."

Malakai turned away from Keeva to look at her, concern in his always watchful eyes. Something in her face must have spooked him, because his gaze narrowed, and he pulled out his phone.

Keeva turned to speak as Jasmine slid into her seat, but Jasmine got there before she could say a thing. "It's okay. I know you want to offer to go, but it's okay, Keeva. Kai will only tell you after. You might as well stay."

Jasmine drummed her fingers anxiously on the table, tensing when the elevator opened to reveal Zeke. The vampire was pulling a tee on over his torso, his eyes tired as he glanced at Malakai.

"Why the summons?"

"Jasmine would like to speak to us all. Did you see Dylan on your way?"

Zeke shook his head, taking his own seat and a mug of blood that Keeva handed him. The elevator came to life again, and Dylan strode in, fully dressed and wide awake as he sipped an energy drink. He wore a Sicarius tee and cargo pants but no shoes, his long blond hair pulled back into a ponytail.

"I know why I'm up at this ungodly hour, but why the hell are you guys?"

Jasmine watched as Malakai raised both his brows, then his eyes slipped to Jasmine as Dylan strode over and took the seat next to her. Panic flared in her chest again, and she felt cool fingers slip into hers, squeezing before she heard Dylan say, "It's okay, Jazz. It will be okay."

Jasmine heard herself laugh, the sound bitter as she pulled her fingers from Dylan's and shook her head. "I don't think it will, Dylan. I'm not sure it will."

Dylan started to talk to her, but she ignored him until everyone had taken a seat, and then she could not find the words to begin. Where did you start to tell your brothers that your selfish act is the reason why their brother died? How do you tell them that their only sister had lied for centuries because she was afraid of losing them?

Maybe this was her destiny. Maybe she was meant to lose everything. There was a reason why her ancestors made seers stay isolated, kept them from interacting with most people for this very purpose. Had they not been ambushed that day, she would have been sequestered on her first bleeding and she would have lost her brothers.

Maybe it was better for someone like her to never know love, never know what it was like to have the simple pleasures. She should have never gone looking for them after the slaughter. She should never have tried to figure out how to break the sleeping curse and should have just stayed asleep.

Then, perhaps, she might have salvaged a sliver of her foolish heart.

"Jesus Christ, Jazz. You need to let out the pain or you will snap."

Jasmine flung up her walls to protect herself from Dylan's empathic powers as she looked up to see her family watching her with careful eyes. They all watched her with this expectancy, with such love that it made this even harder to do.

And by the gods, she wished Roman was here to give her strength.

"I … I …" Jasmine stuttered, shaking her head as she hid behind her hands for a second, a whisper in her mind as she listened.

The truth to vanquish your guilt. The truth to remove the shackles. The truth is the path to love.

"What do you feel guilty for, Jazz? Please, you can tell us anything."

Malakai's voice was calm and reassuring, and Jasmine knew she couldn't say the words.

"I need to show you."

Jasmine held out her hands, with Malakai taking hold of one and Dylan the other until everyone at the table was holding hands, and then Jasmine lowered her shields and showed them the source of her guilt. She showed them what she had shown Zeke when they had first met and the events leading up to it, parts she had even kept from Zeke when showing him their past.

She stood watching as the human hoisted up the fence and managed to secure it in place, his grunt the only indication that the wind and the effort cost him anything. She had fought the compulsion to pass by this area again, for it was not the time to welcome her brother into the fold. Her visions had told her that this teen, once he was a man, would become as important to her as her brothers, as if despite the fact that their parentage was different, Jasmine knew Ezekiel Collins was meant to be theirs.

The compulsion had started not after Dante had been killed, as she had pretended, but long before, and she had come to visit Ezekiel many times before, bucking against her visions, against the warnings. And then Dante had been killed. Her loss and grief sending her away from Dylan and Malakai because her vision of his death had not come soon enough to save him. She could not have her remaining brothers hate her for it.

She had stopped to feed, grabbing some apples to keep her going along with blood on her journey, when she had come across a small child crying in a barn, the welts on his arms making the predator in her rise to the surface.

She had intended to speak to the boy, yet a vision of the child as a man, a vampire, stole the time from her, and when she returned to herself, he had gone back inside. Jasmine left with a heavy heart, wanted to steal the boy away and raise him as her own until he became one of them, yet she knew she could not, for he deserved to see the sun, to feel it upon his skin, to live as he should before his human life was taken from him.

Yet that did not stop her from altering many a journey so that she could check up on him.

Over time, the boy turned into a gangly teen, then a stocky, well-built young man. She could almost feel his strength as he lifted a wooden pole and hammered it into the ground. From her hideout in the branches of a tree, Jasmine watched Ezekiel until she heard a crack, a branch from a tree above him snapping in the storm, and though she had not meant to interfere, she could not sit by and do nothing.

Zeke ducked and stumbled backwards, landing in the dirt as Jasmine landed under the branch and tossed it aside with little effort. Spinning around at Zeke's shocked gasp, Jasmine held out her hand to him, pulling him up when his warm fingers slipped into hers.

It felt right …

"Are you an angel?" the young man asked, his eyes wide with wonder.

Jasmine smiled, shaking her head. "I am not. I am family. Or I will be soon enough."

Jasmine turned to go but stopped when she felt a hand on her arm. "Don't go."

And she did not want to. She wanted to make the mother who beat him with her belt know what it felt like to have the leather against her flesh. She wanted to make the father who ridiculed the boy feel the pain it caused his son. But her vision had been clear.

In order for Ezekiel Collins to be ready, he needed to carry the weight of darkness within him, and nothing Jasmine could do would alter the course of destiny. She had already interfered enough, long before she was supposed to, and fate knew how she would be punished for it.

Instead, Jasmine faced the young man, her eyes turning red as she erased the memory of their meeting from the human's mind, her heart hurting as she vanished into the trees, watching as he continued with his work, oblivious to her watchful eye from a distance.

Her mind drifted back to the warnings, when her visions told her that going to Ezekiel before the time was right would start a chain of events that she could not stop. Jasmine had been foolish, cocky to think she could defy destiny. She had been warned that one of her brothers would die, and still, she had not held back.

The memory pushed into her mind, and she let the pain wash over her.

Panic welled inside her as she darted through the forest, her muscles burning, and she knew if she still had to breathe, her lungs would be on fire. Her brothers, Malakai and Dylan, kept pace beside her as Jasmine scanned her eyes back and forth, hoping, praying that she had not been the one who sealed her brother's fate by ignoring the path chosen by the gods.

She stumbled over her own footing as images of Dante plagued her, his screams of agony shredding her non-beating heart as she urged her other brothers forward.

I have been selfish, and in finding one brother, I have condemned another. *She had seen visions of their future brother Ezekiel for years now, and she had fought against her curiosity to go and see him for herself. The voices in her head had whispered to her, telling her that it was not time yet to go to Ezekiel, yet Jasmine had defied them, thinking she knew better than beings who had gifted her with visions of other people's destiny from when she was a young child.*

And when she defied them, it had sent a ripple along her own future, and now, after bearing witness to the torment and torture of their oldest brother, Dante, her and Malakai's blooded brother, Jasmine had been filled with dread.

They had been told that Dante had been captured by a rival Kiss, and she could still smell the scent of the fire, the burnt flesh, as she offered herself up to the gods in place of her brother.

Time seemed to stall on its axis, the world around them frozen as Jasmine came face-to-face with a cloaked figure who clutched a staff and looked at her with skeletal features and eyes as white as a dove.

"You have dismissed the gift we have bestowed upon you. You have thought yourself a better judge than we."

Jasmine dropped to one knee, bowing her head. "I was foolish, weak. I implore you to punish me and not Dante for my actions."

"It serves us not to punish you. Losing your brother and living with your actions will be punishment enough. We need you as you are ... the other is merely collateral damage."

Time sped up once more, and then she was moving, suddenly on her feet, tears running down her face as they stumbled into the home where they once were born and Jasmine let loose a strangled sob as she caught sight of Dante's sword in the dirt, his cloak still smouldering as ash fluttered about in the wind.

Jasmine fell to her knees, her palms resting on the burnt edges of Dante's cloak. "This is all my fault. I have caused this."

Malakai rested his hand on her shoulder and squeezed. "You did not see this coming until it was already too late. If we were meant to save him, you would have envisioned it earlier. Dante chose the path he walked upon. His death is not your fault."

Jasmine wanted to scream at him that yes, it was her fault. She had started this, and had she not gone to see the teenager at the farm, then Dante would not be nothing more than dust or ash. They might not have agreed with Dante a lot of the time, but he was their brother, and as if it were Jasmine's own hand that had burned him, she felt the guilt of it like an anchor that threatened to drag her under the water.

They can never know the truth. I can never tell them I could have prevented this.

Jasmine dropped her hands, a sob retching from her as tears trickled down her cheeks, her eyes remaining shut as she dared not see her brothers' reactions. She cried because she had not fully grieved the loss, that even though Dante's blood was not on her hands, she had the chance to stop the killing blow and Jasmine had chosen her curiosity over the love of her family.

And she had been so relieved when it had not been Dylan or Malakai who had been killed.

"Jasmine."

She lifted her blue eyes to meet Malakai's, shocked at the abundance of love that shone in his eyes. He reached out and cupped her cheek, a small smile on his lips.

"You are not responsible for Dante's death. He was the master of his own destiny. His own decisions led him on his path. If you were meant to prevent his death, then no choice you could have made would have stopped that. This guilt is not yours to carry. Let it go."

Jasmine shook her head, frowning. "How can you say that? Was Dante a bit of a dick? Sure. But I was too far away when I had the vision to stop it. I chose Ezekiel, and we lost Dante."

Dylan snorted, rolling his eyes. "Jazz, Dante pissed off a lot of people. He didn't play nice with others. I loved him, but he was never happy with his life. He hated that being made a vampire put him at the bottom of the power structure. Hell, even when we were human, he despised how much power we had. I knew he was jealous, and I said nothing."

"If you carry this guilt, then it is all of ours to carry," Malakai said. "I knew he planned to double-cross the vampires he ran with, and I didn't offer to help. As Dylan said, Dante was never happy with his lot. He did not want to work to better himself. He lived a lot longer than I expected him to."

Jasmine blinked at the stark honesty in Malakai's tone, looking from Malakai to Dylan, then her eyes landed on Zeke, who watched her carefully before he spoke. "Do you blame me for the loss of your visions?"

"Of course not!" she exclaimed, wanting to hug him and take that sadness from his eyes.

Malakai patted her cheek. "You did not have to hide this from us, Jasmine. None of us can say we ever made the right decision every time faced with it. We love you. We always will. That will never change."

Malakai pulled her out of the chair and into an embrace, then she felt Dylan join in the hug as Zeke rested his hand on her shoulder. Jasmine cried, feeling the weight being lifted from her soul as she let herself believe that everything would be okay.

CHAPTER NINETEEN

Roman

ROMAN HADN'T LEFT LIKE JASMINE THOUGHT HE HAD.

Instead, he lingered on the edges of the forest, staying downwind so she would not catch his scent, and watched the cabin for the entire day, fighting against the rage and bitterness inside him and feeling like an absolute dick for making Jasmine cry.

Roman had thought he had left that part of him behind, the little boy who was rejected by his father, had witnessed the hell his mother had gone through. He had been to enough therapy sessions after a deployment that he knew it was PTSD, and that never had an expiry date. It crept up when you least expected it to and kicked you square in the ass.

If he was being honest with himself, Roman couldn't handle being rejected by Jasmine, having her see the faults in him, and knowing he wasn't good enough for her, which of course he wasn't.

Seeing his father again had rattled him more than he wanted to admit, and he had taken his anger out on Jasmine, which wasn't fair at all. Yet she hadn't been able to come clean about her own feelings, and Roman knew he did not want to end up feeling the same white-hot rage for Jasmine that he did with his father.

When Dylan had collected Jasmine, he fought to go to her, even as she lingered for just a little before being resigned to the fact that Roman wasn't coming back anytime soon. He had waited long enough for them to leave, then lost himself to the forest for a day or two, delaying the inevitable gut punch that would floor him. When he was exhausted and hungry, he returned to the cabin and went inside, caught a hint of Jasmine's scent, and after shoving some clothes in his backpack, Roman locked up the cabin and high-tailed it out of there, unable to be in his once place of solitude that would now always remind him of his time with Jasmine.

And then there was work.

Roman loved his job at Sicarius Security. He even enjoyed working at Dante's. Malakai was a decent boss, and he and Dylan had the same tactical minds. But he had been brutally honest with Jasmine when he said he couldn't stand by and watch her with anyone else.

Roman wasn't entirely sure he would ever recover from Jasmine Cavanagh.

He had driven to Conor and Abbie's; however, he had not gone inside. Instead, he had lain down on one of the tables and just stared up at the sky, at the moon, and tried to calm the turmoil in his head.

But all he could think about was her.

The door to the pub opened, and Conor leaned in the doorway after letting a steady stream of punters in the door. "If you think I'm feeding you after you've lain about all evening doing sweet fuck all, you're sadly mistaken. Stop being a grumpy ass and pull a few pints behind the bar."

Huffing out a breath, Roman sat up, grabbed his bag, and headed inside the busy bar. A few Inferna greeted him, but Roman headed straight to the bar and kept his mind busy. The routine of it took his thoughts from Jasmine, yet all it took was a smart remark from Ezra, who had come into the bar already drunk, to snap the taut elastic of Roman's temper.

"Glad to hear you found sense and dumped the uppity

bitch," Ezra said with a smirk, and it only took a second for Roman to have the other wolf yanked upright, and then there were fists flying. Glass crashed to the ground as Roman shoved him backwards, Ezra knocking into a table, and then Roman lunged, skidding to a stop when Abbie got in between them and yelled.

"Enough!" Her voice had dropped to a rough growl, and Abbie's eyes flashed with amber. "You—get in the kitchen and take your anger out on the pots and pans while Conor deals with Ezra."

Roman made to argue, but it only took one glare for him to make his way to the back room, and despite the mountain of dishes and pots, he was delighted to be out of the way. Abbie and Conor said nothing as they brought glasses and plates back, ignoring Roman's grumble when he said that this was why people purchased dishwashers.

An hour slipped by with Roman mindlessly washing more dishes than they had patrons, and he was beginning to think that Abbie and Conor were just making work for him to do. He stopped only to drink the beer that Conor brought him and eat the burger that Abbie forced him to.

Roman wasn't sure what he was going to do about things. He had to explain to Jasmine how her reluctance to be up front about them made him feel, even if he felt like a soppy SOB doing so. He wanted Jasmine to be his. He wanted people to know she was his and be damned if any other male tried to put their hands on her.

He knew he had lusted over Jasmine since he first laid eyes on her, felt the acerbic bite of her smart mouth, and once he had a taste of her, that was it for him. Both man and wolf were in agreement that they wanted Jasmine as theirs.

The feisty vampire had dug her way into his home, his bed, and Roman knew that he would never be able to feel the same sense of peace or serenity in the cabin without her.

Hiro popped his head in the door, waving a white flag

with a grin, and stepped inside, the kitsune motioning with his head to the door. "You have a visitor."

He hated himself for the dart of hope that punched him in the gut, but Hiro's face fell. "Sorry, Ro. It isn't her, but your visitor is more my type than yours. You want me to send him back?"

Roman grunted out a response, turning back to the task at hand as Hiro held open the door and Malakai Cavanagh strode in, dressed in an impeccable suit, his handsome face amused as Hiro roamed his eyes over the vampire and muttered about how it was such a shame he was taken.

Malakai chuckled, smiling at Hiro as he said, "Yes, a shame. However, my Keeva would break both our handsome faces if I flirt with you."

Hiro's face went bright red, and he dashed out the door, leaving Roman alone with the Primus of the Irish vampires. Malakai Cavanagh appeared as the rich CEO of his multinational company, a man who liked expensive suits and fast cars, and had a contingent of human and Inferna in tears because he had found Keeva. And while he looked like a pretty boy in a suit, Malakai was a calculating, shrewd businessman who wasn't afraid to get his hands dirty.

"First the kitsune, now you?" Malakai offered as he walked around to the sink where Roman stood. "Perhaps I should go out more without Keeva for all the compliments."

Roman narrowed his gaze as Malakai simply smiled and tapped the side of his head.

"Oh, for fuck sake, not you too."

That made Malakai chuckle as Roman shook his head and went back to washing the last of the dishes. He was taken aback as Malakai took off his suit jacket, rolled up the sleeves of his black shirt, and began to dry as Roman washed. They continued in relative silence until they had completed the task.

Roman leaned his hip on the side of the sink. "It's not every day your former boss comes to hand you your P45."

"I hadn't realized you had handed in your notice." The vampire's tone was dry, leading Roman to think that Keeva was having an influence on her fiancé.

"I wasn't planning to, but why else would you be here? With everything ..."

Malakai dried his hands and grabbed his suit jacket. "I think this conversation requires alcohol."

Roman dried his hands and followed Malakai out, spotting Isolde sitting by the door, her unique appearance drawing admiring gazes from the few patrons that remained. Malakai walked to the farthest corner of the room and to the table where none of them would have to sit with their back to the entrance.

Abbie came over, and Roman introduced them. The vampire shook Abbie's hand and told her he was looking forward to having a chat with her next month. Roman ordered a pint, Malakai asking for the same, and that made Abbie's eyebrows raise.

They waited until Abbie had returned with their pints, then left them to their own devices.

"I usually do not interfere in my family's personal affairs, but that did not work out well for Jasmine the last time, and I cannot stand by and watch her retreat into herself again."

Roman leaned back in his chair and looked at Malakai. "Listen, I appreciate that you are looking out for your sister, but I am nothing like that fucker who made her feel like less than herself. Jasmine made her choice of her own free will. I have to accept that."

"And what if I said that what Jasmine really wants is for someone to fight for her? What if I told you that there was a reason for her reluctance?" Malakai asked before taking another sip of his drink.

"I can't fight for something knowing she doesn't want it. There would be no going back for me."

"Ah," Malakai said with a knowing smile. "I am right. She is your mate."

"That doesn't matter, does it? Jasmine doesn't want me."

Malakai slouched in his chair, resting his left leg on his right. "Jasmine was treated like royalty among our people, for she was the one who told of where the path of greatest resistance would come from, when the rain would fall, and when we would be ambushed. Then the vampires came and myself, Dylan, and our brother Dante were changed. Everyone but Jasmine was slaughtered."

Malakai paused as if thinking of the past hurt him, and Roman was about to tell him he did not have to go on when the vampire started speaking again. "Jasmine found us, having grown into a warrior. She demanded that we make her a vampire, and I did so reluctantly. Her visions became more powerful, so we kept them a secret."

Malakai glanced around, then his dark eyes honed in on Roman, holding his gaze. The alpha wolf in him would not make him lower his gaze, even as Malakai smiled. "I think my sister thought she could only be loved if she was the perfect person, the princess she had been when she was human. Thorpe made her feel like that, at the start, until it became clear that his plans were to ensnare Jasmine to get closer to me. Dylan was the only one who saw through it, and it caused friction between my siblings."

"You never see past the public image. My father made everyone think he was the perfect leader, but in private, he was nothing more than an abuser."

"Indeed," Malakai agreed with Roman. "However, I have seen her blossom and grow since she escaped his clutches, and she has never seemed more like her old self than when she was trading barbs with you. I think she needs someone like you, Roman. Someone who will challenge her but let her fly herself, always there to catch her should she falter. A man who will push her out of the way of a speeding car."

Roman reached out and lifted his drink to his lips, his throat suddenly dryer than the Sahara Desert. "While I appreciate the endorsement, Malakai, and I really do, Jasmine needs to make the decision to be with me. I put my cards on the table, and she said she wanted to keep it a secret. I'm not that guy."

The corner of Malakai's lips quirked. "Convince her. I had to convince Keeva that we would work. Thankfully, Scarlett managed to convince Ezekiel. I know what you planned, and I do love my sister; however, she would be an absolute idiot to still have doubts after she sees what you did."

"You'll have to let me know how it goes?"

Malakai drained the rest of his drink and stood. "I expect to see you at Dante's, and if you need that to be an order from your boss, it can be."

Roman ground his teeth together, then let his anger flash in his eyes before he stood, offering Malakai his hand. The vampire shook it, holding his fingers a little tighter as he gave Roman a feral smile. "Make no mistake: I may like you, but you hurt my sister, and I will bury you where no one can find you. I know your tells."

Then Malakai winked, and Roman laughed. "And I know yours, boss. And I would never hurt her."

"Good. I'll settle the bar. I will see you tomorrow night."

Malakai slipped on his suit jacket before heading to the bar, the vampire giving his friends an easy smile before he headed toward Isolde. The Inferna inclining her head to Roman before she ushered Malakai outside, and then it was like a tension burst in the room and Abbie was in front of him asking him a mountain of questions.

"He really is as handsome and polite as he appears on TV.

And he was drinking a beer? Oh my god, Roman! We didn't have anything fancier."

Roman rolled his eyes as Conor needled his wife about finding Malakai attractive. Grabbing his keys and his bag, Roman offered a wave in goodbye, and then he was in his car and driving back toward the city, bypassing the exit and headed as if he were driving toward Killarney.

He steered the car off the main road, careful to stay outside of pack lands, and pulled his car over at the end of the mountain. He turned off the engine, getting out, the bite of cold night air sobering him even as it wrapped around him with a familiarity that he once knew.

Roman scaled the mountain, his muscle memory reminding him where to reach for the grooves with his fingers, his boots seamlessly finding the old familiar rocks to climb up. It took him less than ten minutes to scale the cliffside, then Roman sat down on the edge and waited.

His eyes went down to the smoke that billowed out from the trees, the only indication that any life interrupted the woods. When his father had thrown him out, Roman had gone gladly, his mother long since lost to the wild. Now, looking down on the place where he had grown up, remembering the pain and the horrific actions of his father, Roman wanted to kill him.

But as much as his father deserved to die, Roman would not be the one to dole out that justice. He remembered what his mother had once said to him, huddled in his room, after one of his father's rages.

"Don't cry, my love. It will be all right."

"I will kill him," Roman snarled, *wishing more than ever that he had a wolf's claws and teeth. His nails lengthened, his teeth also, but pain rippled through him as he couldn't complete the change.*

His mother took his face in her hands. "No, my love. I will be the one to tear him limb from limb when I know that you are safe. Once you are, once I am certain that we can get away, then I will kill him."

Roman sucked in a breath because his father had discovered their plans and then, then she had been brutalized. And before he knew it, his mother was lost to the wild.

Roman heard a snuffle, the sound of paws against the dirt as a wolf with golden eyes padded cautiously toward him. He let her inhale his scent, take the time to remember who he was and what he was, before Roman turned to look at the other wolf, letting amber flash in his gaze before he smiled.

"Hey, mam, it's me, Roman."

The wolf tilted her head as Roman held out his hand, palm down. The wolf sniffed before she hit his palm with her head, letting Roman pat her on the head before she took a step back.

"I know it's been a while, but I wanted to tell you that I'm good. I'm happy. Or at least I think I will be. There's this girl."

The wolf lay down on the ground, her eyes on him, so Roman continued. "She is funny and sarcastic and drop-dead gorgeous, and even though she isn't sure about me, I'm sure about her. Maybe one day, I can bring her to meet you. I think you would like her."

A howl sounded in the distance. His mother's ears twitched as she dragged her gaze from Roman and toward the wild wolves that had been his mother's family for as long as Abbie, Conor, Tyler, Hiro, Réiltín, and even bloody Ezra had been his. The same blood might run through their veins, but they would never again be the same.

Roman offered his mother a smile. "It's okay, mam. Go to your family. I just wanted you to know that I'm okay now. That asshole hasn't ruined me, he set me free. I have a family, and I am about to go tell the woman I love that I love her. I'm not going to let him make me afraid of her rejecting me."

The wolf came over and nudged his hand, then danced away, stopping to look back at him. She lifted her muzzle to the sky and howled. The wolves in the wild answered her call, and Roman did as well, feeling the song in his blood before his mother took off at a run and vanished from view.

Roman stayed where he was for a little while longer, watching as the sun rose in the sky as he formulated a plan.

Jasmine Cavanagh was his mate, and he wasn't going to let her go without a fight.

CHAPTER TWENTY

Jasmine

"YOU ARE COMING OUT WITH US TONIGHT, AND I'M NOT TAKING no for an answer."

Jasmine had argued with Dylan, telling him she was in no need of a party, that all she wanted to do was curl up in bed with a rom-com and eat her weight in ice cream. Dylan had rolled his eyes, telling her that he knew she missed being at Dante's and since the place would be closed to the public, she could just relax. Dylan had argued that even Zeke and Scarlett were making an appearance so she could get all dressed up and stop moping as he went into her wardrobe and tossed her gold sparkly dress on the bed.

And that was how she ended up dressed in her New Year's Eve dress, sat beside Dylan as they pulled in outside Dante's. She had decided to make an effort on the off chance Roman would show up, her dress just hitting her thighs, her heels making her as tall as Dylan, and she knew she looked good.

Jasmine had held her tongue for the duration of the car ride, but as the door was opened for them to get out, Jasmine grabbed Dylan's elbow.

"Is he coming?"

"I dunno, Jazz. He was invited."

She knew her face couldn't hide her disappointment, but she changed the subject. "I never said sorry for not believing you about Colin."

Dylan smiled and leaned over to kiss her cheek. "It's all good, sis. I knew what you were feeling, so I know it was more what you wanted to feel rather than how I made you feel. All I want is for you to be happy. We all do. And if Roman makes you happy, then go for it."

Dylan escorted her to the doors of Dante's, his hand on her arm as they went up the steps, the lights off until they were standing on the top step. Suddenly, the lights blazed to life, and Jasmine sucked in a shocked breath.

Dante's had been transformed into a festival of holidays that made joy dance inside her heart. Her DJ booth had been transformed into a winter wonderland, with a Santa's grotto, complete with fake snow and a mechanical reindeer. A wind machine made the snow flutter into the air, falling like snowflakes.

At the bottom of the stairs hung a banner that said "Happy New Year," with a champagne fountain and sparklers. It even had a disco ball hanging over the bar like the one she had planned on getting.

She laughed at the sight of the Halloween corner in the darkest corner of the dance floor, with bats fluttering in the air, a cauldron filled with mist and magic, and enough sweets to rot your teeth.

It was all the holidays she had missed all rolled into one, and it delighted her as Jasmine clambered down the stairs and threw her arms around Malakai, who was dressed in a pair of slacks and a black shirt.

"Oh my god, Malakai. I can't believe you did all this for me!"

Malakai glanced at Keeva, who was dressed in a black dress and matching Converse, as she grinned at Jasmine with a shrug. "We were only invited. No idea who set this all up."

Zeke came over after settling Scarlett in a seat. Isolde sitting across from the succubus with that scowl of hers. The music started, and some of the Sicarius employees started to step onto the dance floor.

Jasmine glanced at Dylan, who winked. "My only task was to get you here. Mission completed." He snagged a beer from one of the ice buckets and headed toward Scarlett.

Jasmine was utterly confused, wondering who would have gone to all this effort for her if not for her brothers. She glanced at Zeke; the other vampire cleared his throat as he offered Jasmine an explanation.

"None of us thought of what you may have missed when you were sleeping. But we all came together to make it happen. That wolf of yours ran it like a military operation. I think even Dylan was impressed with how he worked to put this all together so quickly."

Roman had done this. Roman had known she was sad to have missed all her favourite holidays, and sometime between all the time they spent together and when she had dissed and dismissed him, Roman had cared enough to offer her this sliver of happiness.

And she had pushed him away.

"He did all this for me? I pushed him away. I said awful things to him."

Keeva stepped forward, hesitating for a second before she put her hand on Jasmine's arm, as if she forgot that Jasmine had the same immunity to her kiss of death powers as Malakai did, then she smiled. "I tried to run from Malakai. I didn't think we fit. I didn't consider myself in his league, but he wasn't deterred. I think he liked that I didn't back down."

"If it had not been for Scarlett, for her not giving up on me, I would not be as happy as I am now. If Roman truly has feelings for you, then he will not let you drive him away," Zeke offered, then walked back to his pregnant succubus.

Keeva thrust a drink into her hand, then told her it was time to party like it was New Year's Eve. The music was turned up a notch, and Jasmine tried to push thoughts of a certain wolf out of her mind as she danced with Keeva. And despite the fact she should have been in her element, her heart and soul felt like something, or rather someone, was missing.

She went to the bar to get herself a drink, smiling when Dylan slid up to her and nudged her shoulder. "I'm gonna head out with Scarlett. Me and Isolde will take her home so Zeke can have a rest."

"Not like you to leave the party first, Dylan. Are you okay?"

Dylan winked at her. "I'm good, little sister. I've just realized that I don't want Grayce to grow up seeing me in the states I get. I want to stop drinking myself to oblivion and all that. Being around Scarlett makes me feel happy. I know it's not my happiness, but I take what I can get." Dylan frowned, then began to talk again. "Roman made you happy. I know you're scared, but isn't falling in love supposed to be a little scary?"

"I ruined it, bro. I went full vapid Jasmine and pretended he didn't matter to me. What if he never forgives me?"

"You won't know until you try. Night, Jazz, love you. He looks damn good."

Dylan inclined his head, and Jasmine turned slowly in that direction, her eyes clashing with hazel as Roman fidgeted with the sleeve of his tailored suit. Gone was the rough and ready wolf with a penchant for plaid, and replaced was a dangerously sexy wolf in a suit of black. Of course, there was no tie, and the buttons to his shirt were popped at the neck. His long brown hair had been cut and slicked back and his beard trimmed to a neat stubble.

Everyone else in the room vanished as she walked toward him, the wolf self-conscious as some of his work colleagues whistled as Roman descended the steps. Jasmine didn't like the way the other women watched Roman with a new appreciation, undressing him with their eyes, and Jasmine felt a possessive growl ripple from her lips.

Roman studied her with an amused expression, stopping on the dance floor as someone rang a bell behind the bar and shouted that the countdown to New Year's was happening.

"I can't believe you did all this for me ... even when ... I mean." Jasmine stumbled over her words as a slow smile tugged at the corners of Roman's mouth.

"If you thought I was gonna give up that easy, Jasmine Cavanagh, then you don't know me at all."

Heat licked at her skin, her body thrumming with antici-pation, craving his touch and his closeness, but still, Roman kept a comfortable distance between them.

"Why are you here, Roman?" Jasmine asked as someone started counting down from ten.

"Because you deserved to be kissed by someone who loves you on New Year's."

Roman cupped her face in his hands, as everyone laughed and shouted Happy New Year, he lowered his full lips to hers and claimed her mouth for himself, a possessive melding of lips and tongue and teeth, the world fading away as Roman kissed her in front of everyone and she let him.

Her hands gripped his shirt, holding him to her until he pulled back, inhaling a breath, her lipstick smeared on his lips. Jasmine reached up with her thumb, rubbing his lower lip as the music changed, and he nudged her to the dance floor, his hands on her waist as she rested her head on his chest.

"I'm sorry. For what I said. I was afraid. A while ago, someone told me I would fall for a wolf like no other and it might kill me. I didn't want to die, but I don't want to miss out on us because I was afraid."

"I let seeing my father spook me. It raked over some inse-curities I had, and when I thought you were ashamed of being with me, I lashed out. We both played a part in it, darling."

Jasmine lifted her head, arching up to kiss him. "I believe that was our first proper fight. I expect lots of makeup sex."

"Yes, Ma'am." Roman's growl curled her toes as Jasmine took his head and led him to one of the seating areas. Roman sat down first and pulled her into his lap.

"Where do we go from here?" Jasmine asked, wanting to know what the future held.

"Well, I was hoping to get you naked, but I don't think that's what you are asking."

Jasmine chuckled at the husky tone and rolled her eyes. "I meant what do you want, for us, for our future?"

Roman pondered her question for a second, then ran his tongue over his lips. "I want to be with you, Jazz. You are it for me. My Mate. I've felt it for a while, maybe even back to the first time we met. I want to be your partner, like Abbie is for Conor. I want to be what you need me to be."

"I'm stubborn and prone to react."

"I know all that. But I'm stubborn too," Roman admitted as he tucked a strand of hair behind her ear, his other hand on the bare skin of her thigh. "I love you, Jasmine."

His words hung in the air, and she swallowed, feeling like something was shifting inside her, this burst of happiness she had not felt before making tears well in her eyes as she realized that it was okay not to know what the future held. It was okay not knowing what might happen.

Right now, Jasmine had a man who loved her, who didn't try to cage her, who let her spread her wings and would be there to catch her if she fell. This was what she had been searching for her entire life and now, whatever the future might bring, if she had Roman, then everything would be okay.

"I love you, too. But I think the hair will need some getting used to."

Roman blinked at her words, like he was surprised to hear her say them. "It'll grow back." And then he was kissing her, his fingers digging into her flesh as she met him stroke for stroke, kiss for kiss, each press of lips cementing their bond until Jasmine wanted out of her dress, out of the club, and into a bed.

Hell, she'd settle for the storeroom at this stage.

As if sensing her thoughts, Roman broke the kiss and grinned. "I need to take my mate home."

"I think tonight might be the time to experiment with the collar and leash," Jasmine retorted with a smirk, and Roman chuckled, getting to his feet and dragging her out of the club, Keeva cat-calling after them as they left through the front door. Roman kissed her again until her head spun. And then she realized it wasn't because of the kiss.

There was none of the pain that usually came with her visions. It was like one minute Roman was kissing her, and then next, the future unfolded in front of her eyes. There was a clarity in her now, and Jasmine was puzzled at how easy it was.

It felt like she had stepped out of her body and watched as Roman called her name, worry in his tone.

"You have accepted that the future is not yours to know. You have accepted the gift we have given you. Abuse it again, and lose the wolf like no other. The witch spoke true, yet your love for him was both an undoing and an awakening. Now, it is time to fully embrace what you are capable of."

Jasmine watched as the vision unfolded, quickly in vivid pictures, and then she was back in her body, bolting down the middle of Patrick's Street, kicking off her heels, the steady presence of Roman by her side as he called Malakai on his phone.

She saw the car wreck as she rounded the corner, watched as Hellhounds dragged an unconscious Dylan along the ground, as Isolde fought like a champion to protect Scarlett, who was crouched by the front of the car, her hands clutching her stomach. A blue-haired creature held out her hand to Scarlett, who looked like she recognised the female talking to her.

The blue-haired female averted her gaze to Jasmine, then she whistled, the hounds letting go of Dylan as one of her companions lifted her brother off the ground and tossed him into the back of a van. The hounds snarled, their drool falling to the ground and hissing.

Roman had pulled a gun and fired off a shot. The blue-haired creature inclined her head as she ducked, moving with the speed of a vampire. The hellhounds blocked her way as Jasmine heard the blue-haired woman say to Scarlett, "Come with me of your own free will, and the others will not be harmed."

She flicked her wrist, and one of the hounds leapt toward Jasmine as Scarlett screamed at the woman to call them back, that she would go.

"Scarlett! No. Wait!" Jasmine yelled at her. The succubus turned to Jasmine the moment the other Inferna helped her to her feet.

"Tell Zeke I love him. Tell Keeva she taught me well. I'll be okay."

Jasmine looked for any way around the hounds as Isolde let loose a scream of fury, steam coming out her nose as one of the Inferna she was fighting hit her with a cheap shot to the back of the head and she went down.

The Inferna helped Scarlett into the van, closed the door, and then she whistled back at the hounds, who returned to their mistress, then clambered into the van. Then the blue-haired Inferna offered the coldest smile Jasmine had ever seen, lifting her hand to the sky, then dropping it.

Jasmine heard the pull back from a sniper rifle, knew in her gut that the bullet was not meant for her, and the Inferna watched as Jasmine's head snapped to look at Roman, and for a moment, Jasmine wondered if fate would be cruel enough to take Roman from her.

She felt her power surge inside her, her eyes slamming shut as a scream ripped from her. The bullet flew through the air as she clenched her fists, screaming and tossing her hands to the side, flinging her palms open.

The road was suddenly drenched in silence. Jasmine snapped her eyes open, an unfamiliar greyish black on the edges of her vision, and her mouth hung open in surprise.

The street was almost frozen, moving with a slowness, with every second feeling like a minute. It was like the world had gone into slow motion, her power making it so, but as she saw her family race around the corner, unable to get through this bubble of time stopped to get to them, Jasmine felt her power waver, so she darted forward and pushed Roman to the ground just as time began to rush forward to catch up with real life.

The bullet hit the ground a second later as exhaustion knocked her to her knees. The van containing Scarlett and Dylan sped off, Zeke running after it until it vanished before their eyes, and Zeke screamed Scarlett's name in a pure agonistic sound.

"What the hell was that, Jazz? Your eyes were fucking black!" Roman growled at her as she gingerly got back to her feet, her wolf grabbing her arm to help steady her as Jasmine tilted sideways.

"I think I just stopped time."

Roman glanced at Malakai. "Did ye know she could do that?"

"How could they! I didn't know I could do that!" Jasmine exclaimed, looking down to where Keeva was checking on Isolde.

Malakai ignored Roman's question, "I need to go to Zeke. Scarlett will be okay. Dylan will protect her."

Roman pulled Jasmine to him, his scent, and his heat

keeping her grounded as she wondered what else her powers could let her do.

"I could have stopped them. I should have. But I couldn't lose you."

Malakai walked a distraught Zeke back to where they stood. A team of Sicarius agents came to examine the car, the scene, as Malakai suggested that they head back home and ready themselves for the next fight.

"He took two of our own. We do not let that go. We tell the Inferna council that the line has been drawn and war has been declared. We cannot solve this without bloodshed. We will no longer take orders; we will give them. The time for politics is over. It's time we go to war."

Malakai clasped Ezekiel on the shoulder. "Dylan would die protecting her. Take solace in the fact they have each other. Dylan will move heaven and earth to bring your Scarlett back to you. He will give his life to protect them both."

Zeke wore this wrecked expression that made Jasmine well up, glancing at her hands, wondering if she could stop time again, but nothing happened, and she hoped that Malakai's words wouldn't need to come true.

Dylan will be okay. He has to be … and so will Scarlett and Grayce.

Jasmine pushed down the sinking feeling in her stomach as she locked eyes with Malakai, and her brother shook his head, urging her to keep her thoughts to herself.

CHAPTER TWENTY-ONE

Jasmine

JASMINE TOOK THE BRUNT OF MALAKAI'S PUNCH TO HER shoulder, growling as she yet again failed to manifest the time-stopping powers she had two nights ago when trying to save Roman's life. She had tried everything to replicate the surge of power, from meditating to spending time researching in Zeke's library, to no avail.

Now Malakai was using another tactic to try and bring her surprise power back. When no one could sleep, because they were missing two of their own, Malakai wanted to spar, but he wanted to see if Jasmine could stop his advancement with her power.

Jasmine had wanted to tell Kai they had bigger things to think about, but Kai had told her that Keeva was beside herself over Scarlett, and he wanted to distract her from her pain.

Malakai grabbed Jasmine under her arm and tossed her over his shoulder, with them both landing on their backs. Malakai rolling up with a grin.

Jasmine lay on the ground for half a minute, staring at the ceiling. She was angry at herself, angry at the universe for screwing them over. She had tried several times to get her powers to work, and she hadn't even had a vision.

Malakai held out his hand to help her up, and she slapped it away, rolling to her knees with a growl. "This is not fucking helping."

Malakai moved, ignoring her frustration as he came at her, elbowing her in the stomach with enough force to knock the air from her lungs and make her anger snap.

"Enough!" Jasmine yelled, and then she felt the same sense of nothing, a deafening silence as Malakai recoiled his arm to strike at her again. Jasmine felt the power in her falter so she took a step to the side and cocked out her foot. The magic in her yanked back so hard it caused her to hiss, but then Malakai was tripping over her foot and face-planting to the ground.

Her brother groaned as he lifted himself up with just his arms and then jumped to his feet, proving he was no slouch. He turned to Jasmine with his brow arched. "You were saying?"

"Shut your face, know-it-all. You made me so mad, but what did it prove? That I can't control it. That when we really need me to be a badass, I have performance anxiety."

That dragged a chuckle from Keeva that had the siblings looking at the banshee, who waved her hand. "Sorry, mind went to the gutter. Please continue."

Malakai grinned at his fiancé, then sobered. "Your power flares when your emotions are heightened. You were scared when you stopped it the first time, and you were angry this time. Once you know what triggers it, you can master it."

"So, what, you're gonna stand around all day making an ass of yourself and keep trying to make me angry? That's bullshit, Kai."

Malakai took a step back from Jasmine, yet his eyes were over his shoulder. Jasmine turned to see Keeva and Roman on their feet, Keeva advancing on Roman, her palms outstretched.

"That won't work. I know Keeva won't hurt Roman."

Keeva looked at Jasmine with an expression that served her well as the assassin known as Death. "Jazz, I would make him vomit blood if it meant getting Scarlett back." Keeva dragged her gaze back to Roman. "I'll try and not make it hurt too much."

Jasmine screamed as Keeva reached for Roman, the world slowing and spluttering as her body weakened, but she managed to get between her wolf and her future sister-in-law. As quickly as it happened, time returned to normal, and Keeva put her hands on Jasmine's arms.

"Huh. Your eyes went freaky black again." That was all Keeva managed to say as Jasmine pitched her head forward, knocking Keeva back and to the floor.

Malakai was at her side a second later as Keeva rubbed her forehead. "Jesus, Jazz," Keeva said as Malakai helped her to her feet. "Your head is as hard as you are stubborn."

Hands on her hips, Jasmine flashed her fangs. "I'm not sorry. Don't you dare put your hands on my man for a fucking experiment. This is my problem, and I will fucking try and fix it on my terms. You hear me?"

Jasmine expected Keeva to fire back at her, but the banshee just grinned. "My bad, Jazz. Kai, let's go."

Her brother let Keeva lead him out of the gym, and she released a sigh, turning to check on Roman. Her wolf's eyes were amber with a smug smile on his lips. "I like the way you claim me, Jasmine Cavanagh."

He had that hungry wolfish expression on his face, the same one he had this morning when she had stripped off her clothes, crawled onto the bed with her ass in the air, and had crooked her finger over her shoulder at Roman. There had been no foreplay, no waiting, just a rush of need that made her wet and ready as Roman took her from behind, his hand in her hair, his cock thrusting in and out of her as Roman bit down hard on her shoulder, marking her, and she had come apart.

"Jazz."

His growl made her laugh as she shrugged. "I was

promised lots of makeup sex, and there hasn't been enough time."

Roman sighed, running his fingers through his hair. "I was gonna head to the cabin. I could do with a run to settle the wolf. This close to the full moon and I'm on edge."

Jasmine would never have guessed that Roman was on edge because his stance, his presence seemed calm and resolute. Roman had sat with Zeke as they trawled through hours of CCTV footage for a single sighting of the van or the blue-haired woman. Zeke had eaten when he was told to, drank when he was advised to, but he would not be okay until his woman was by his side again and their brother returned.

"I'll go with you," Jasmine offered, wanting to return to the cabin because she didn't want the sadness of her being a fool to be her last memory of it.

"You should stay here in case someone needs you," Roman offered, but Jasmine shook her head.

"They can call me if they need me. We all need to be sharp when the council answers Malakai's threat. Unless we get a lead, worrying will do us no good."

Roman held out his hand to her, and she slipped her fingers into his, Jasmine remembering how right and easy it had felt the first time Roman had held her hand. She couldn't believe that she had almost tossed a grenade into their relationship because she had doubted her feelings.

It was like Roman Lowe was destined to be hers.

On the drive out of the city, having told Malakai where they were going, Jasmine bantered back and forth with Roman, trying to lighten the mood.

"I take it you want to stay with me at Sicarius, right? I love the cabin and all, but that commute every evening would be a bitch."

Roman placed his palm on her thigh. "Not sure I can sleep with all the pink, Jazz. We might need to redecorate."

Jasmine felt herself bristle, feeling like Roman was trying

to change who she was, but then realized she was being irrational and that if Roman was going to start living with her, she needed to make him feel welcome.

"I'm keeping the TV though. I want to be able to, when all this is over, spend a day in bed with you, binge-watching some shows or movies. I'm willing to compromise."

Roman squeezed her thigh with a playful growl. "Then ask me to move in with you, Jasmine."

Jasmine turned in her seat, a smile on her lips. "Roman, I'd like you to move in with me. I want you in my life, as my partner. Please say yes."

His answer was a blistering kiss as the car screeched to a halt outside the cabin, and then Roman yanked her into his lap, his hand slipping into her leggings, and he wasted no time in pushing his finger into her slick folds. Her body felt awash with flames, heating as Roman brought her to the edges of climax and then stopped.

"Run."

His voice was a tone she had never heard before, but Jasmine was on board for whatever came at the end of it. She rocked against his erection; the growl that saturated the air promised Jasmine would pay for driving him this insane. Jasmine nipped at his throat, then pushed open the door, glancing over her shoulder once before she bolted into the forest.

Roman howled. Shivers racking her body. She knew it was werewolf custom to chase a mate, proving your worth by catching them and fucking them on the forest floor. The mating was final because wolves didn't cheat, and Roman wanted to show Jasmine that he was devoted to her.

Jasmine pumped her arms to go faster, the scent of the forest in her lungs as she dodged under branches and jumped over rocks. She was hit by a sudden wave of déjà vu as the vision of her running through the forest flashed in her mind, as something snarled and growled behind her.

Stumbling over her feet as she dared look back, amber eyes blazing through the forest, Jasmine, already sweaty and horny, forgot all about the cliff edge, and suddenly her legs had nowhere to go.

Panic welled in her chest as she tried to reach for her power to slow time.

But she didn't need to.

Roman grabbed her around the waist and slammed her against a nearby tree. His hips surged forward, a pained whimper in his throat as Roman pulled back. "Are you okay?"

Jasmine nodded, letting out a little laugh, then she saw Roman wince. "Babe, what's wrong?"

Every muscle in his jaw clenched as his hand slid down to cup her ass.

"I need to fuck you now."

His voice was animalistic, the wolf very much in his eyes as Jasmine stepped into him, giving him a wolfish grin of her own. "My mate caught me."

Roman's control snapped as he captured her mouth with his, and there was no finesse, no practiced skill, just a wildness that reached inside Jasmine, grabbed hold of her soul as Roman toppled them both to the ground, ripping off her tee and yanking down her leggings right before he freed his cock.

Jasmine groaned as she kicked off her leggings, and then Roman was poised at her entrance, the blunt head of his cock teasing before Roman growled and buried himself to the hilt, Jasmine's back arching in response. Jasmine had to dig her fingers into the dirt as Roman thrust in and out of her with a fever pitch that had her going crazy.

Roman bent her knee back and seemed to thrust deeper into her as she came, hard, her vision blurring. But her mate wasn't done yet.

Roman's teeth grew sharp, his eyes on her shoulder as he kept rotating his hips, sweat on his forehead as Jasmine tilted her head to the side, and that was invitation enough. Jasmine jerked at the feel of Roman's teeth tearing at her skin, then she was screaming as another climax was rung from her, and to stop herself from screaming, she bit her own fangs into Roman's arm.

Her wolf came with a shudder and a growl against her flesh, emptying himself inside her. He collapsed on top of her, breathless, his forehead resting on hers before he rolled, pulling out of her, but pulling her so that she lay in the crook of his arm.

Jasmine curled into his side, looking up at the stars, smiling.

"I think I'm dead," Roman said quietly, causing Jasmine to laugh.

She pulled up his hand and ran her tongue over the wounds on his arm. Her wolf shivered, but not from the cold. Jasmine ran her fingers through his hair, rolling her eyes at the rumble in his chest, then she offered quietly, "I had a vision a long time ago after I was told about the prophecy, about the wolf. It was me running through the forest, being hunted by the wolf, and then I was falling off a cliff. I thought it was my death, but I never saw past the cliff. But it was a vision of this, of you and me, and I just couldn't see it."

Roman rolled so that he faced her, pressing a kiss to her lips. "I'm glad."

Jasmine was surprised at his admission, her lashes lowering before Roman tapped her chin and began to speak. "I'm glad you didn't see me coming because if you had, do you think we would have played the cat and mouse game for so long? If you knew we were evitable, how could you know that what you felt for me was real and not just the way it had to be?"

Frowning, Jasmine shoved him hard. "Ugh, stop making so much sense. It sucks all the fun out of things."

Roman laughed, the sound echoing in the forest. "I didn't

know to expect you, Jasmine, and it knocked the wind out of my sails knowing that I wanted you and thinking you hated me. The first time you kissed me, I was so shell-shocked, but I knew, knew I would die for another taste of you. I cannot believe that we finally got our act together. I never expected to find someone to love me for me."

Roman had sat her down and told Jasmine all about his childhood, his father, and his mother. Jasmine had been ready to cut a bitch for hurting Roman, and that had made Roman grin. She understood now that he had acted out of fear of rejection and that her words had come from her fear as well.

He had told Jasmine that she had a wild heart and it called to him. Roman had whispered words as he loved her, and Jasmine knew that she had been lucky to find Roman.

The wind swept over them, and rain began to trickle from the sky. They dressed quickly, slowly making their way back to the cabin, Roman's arm around her shoulder, and Jasmine felt guilty for feeling so blissfully fucking happy when Dylan and Scarlett were missing.

"They'll be okay. They have to be."

Jasmine opened her mouth to reply. Her feet grinding to a halt as her eyes milked over, and she could see Dylan, huddled in a corner of a cage, his eyes closed, his face bruised and bloody. Jasmine reached for him, wanting to touch him, but he was too far out of her reach.

"The war of hearts has begun. The tide will be set upon its conclusion."

Jasmine shook her head to clear the vision. "I saw Dylan. He's alive. He's locked in a cage somewhere. I could smell damp and magic."

"You need to call Malakai, tell him."

Jasmine waited until they had showered, Roman getting the fire going before she curled up on the couch in one of Roman's T-shirts and video called Malakai.

"How did he look?" Malakai asked as he sat up in bed

rubbing his eyes, and Keeva stirred beside him. Malakai got out of bed and walked to the window. "Did you see Scarlett?"

Jasmine shook her head. "No, just Dylan. He was unconscious, but as far as I could tell, he was alive."

"Let's not tell Ezekiel what you saw right now. You not seeing Scarlett doesn't mean anything, but he will read far too much into it."

They agreed to keep that between themselves for now. Jasmine rising to step outside as she told her big brother, "I feel guilty for smiling. I feel bad for being happy."

"As do I. However, there is a fight coming, Jasmine. We must grab hold of happiness with both hands and hold onto it for dear life. We live in a world where darkness is inevitable. We have to believe that we can overcome, yet we can still enjoy the little slivers of happiness. It is what will keep us going when faced with bloodshed."

Malakai told her he loved her, then hung up. Jasmine must have been standing out in the night for longer than it seemed, because Roman came out and wrapped his arms around her waist, resting his chin on her shoulder. They stayed like that for an age, until the sun threatened to pierce through the clouds and Roman steered her inside.

While Jasmine was outside, Roman had hung a TV over the fireplace, a DVD player hooked up to it. Jasmine turned to look at him, but her wolf just grinned. "You won't get satellite signal this far out, but I managed to grab a few DVDs on my way out. Wanna watch a movie and make out with me?"

Roman wiggled his brows, and Jasmine giggled, shaking her head as she remembered what Malakai had said: We can still enjoy the little slivers of happiness. It is what will keep us going when faced with bloodshed.

Jasmine walked over and pulled Roman down for a kiss. He carried an armful of treats and set them down on the coffee table, and she made herself busy rifling through the stash. He sat down on the couch, and Jasmine snuggled up next to him, happiness in her heart as she leaned back to look at Roman.

"I love you."

He kissed her hard and replied, "I love you too. Does that get me to second base?"

Jasmine laughed as she reached into her back pocket and pulled out a pair of fluffy pink handcuffs. "Definitely more than that, furball."

Amber bled into his eyes as Roman chuckled. "Do your worst, bloodsucker."

Jasmine Cavanagh loved a challenge.

And she loved her wolf.

So when he dared her again to do her worst, Jasmine smiled and did just that.

Turned out, you can make a wolf purr.

CHAPTER TWENTY-TWO

Vindicta

Vindicta watched as Dylan stirred, groaning as he clutched his head, the succubus scooting closer to the vampire in their little cage. She didn't get too close to the bars or the hellhounds that kept sentry, shuffling around the spelled cage where no magic would work. Scarlett had already tried to use her succubus powers to seduce some of the guards and failed.

Dylan groaned again, spitting blood onto the ground as Vindicta looked over at his little pet and raised a brow.

"Did you have to hit him so hard, Callista?"

"He resisted. It was the only way to make him compliant." Her otherworldly accent reminded him of their past, yet he would cut her down if she betrayed him.

The succubus snarled at him. "I won't let you harm my daughter. Her father will come, and he will cut off your balls, and I will watch with glee as he does."

Vindicta stepped closer to the bars. "I have no doubt the obscurum would like to hurt me, and I would like to see him try. It has been such a long time since I felt any pain, I wonder, would he manage it?"

Vindicta reached through the bars to touch the succubus as she shrank back, and a hand grabbed him.

"Don't you dare fucking touch her."

Vindicta snickered, lashing out with his magic and sending Dylan flying back into the bars. The magic in him sent a shiver of ice into his body, and he flinched against it. Tiredness made his bones ache, but though he sensed it, he did not feel it.

"You always were the defender of the weak. You always were the one who wanted to play the hero. It must kill you that the monster got the girl. That everyone around you has fallen prey to their lust and their love and you are still alone. If I had a heart, it would be warmed now."

Dylan brushed his hair from his face and narrowed his gaze, and for a moment, he was happy that his hood and the darkness kept his face hidden.

"You don't know fuck all about me."

He laughed at Dylan's tone. "But that is where you are wrong. I know all about you, Dylan, about Malakai and Jasmine. I even know all about the stray animal you all brought home."

Dylan dragged himself into a sitting position, and he noted how Scarlett moved closer to the vampire. It made him smile. He wanted to shock Dylan ... wanted to see that it had all begun with them all.

Stepping out of the shadows, he lowered his hood. Dylan's eyes widened as he shrank back against the bars so hard they rattled.

He wondered if this was as close to glee as he would ever feel.

"What the hell is going on? You're dead."

The shock in Dylan's tone was worth all the cloak and dagger, the veiled threats, and the mild attacks. The look on Dylan's face was so worth it all.

"You should know by now, dear brother, that sometimes, the dead do not stay that way."

He ignored Scarlett's sharp intake of breath as Dylan surged forward and grabbed the bars.

"Let us out of here. You can't be fuckin' serious."

He lashed out with his magic again and sent Dylan careening back. Blood seeped from a fresh cut on his cheek.

"Callista, let's leave our guests to get comfortable before the fun starts."

He strode out the door with his own little pet following after

him, her hounds of hell standing guard at the door as he listened to
Dylan shout after him.

    "Dante! Dante! Come back here!"

The Sicarius Security series
continues

WAR OF HEARTS

SICARIUS SECURITY BOOK 4

SUSAN HARRIS

Available January 2023

Jasmine

1. Ruelle - Where We Come Alive
2. Rayelle - Trouble's Comin'
3. Icon For Hire - Venom
4. Siiickbrain - PIN CUSHION
5. Sir Spyro - Hell to the Liars
6. AURORA - Running With the Wolves
7. Billie Eilish - bellyache
8. Jennifer Hudson - Burden Down
9. Cemetery Sun - Fake Love
10. Rezz - Falling
11. Tom Grennan - Little Bit of Love
12. Aly & AJ - Slow Dancing
13. Ashnikko - Deal With It (feat. Kelis)
14. Riton - Friday (feat. Mufasa & Hypeman) - Dopamine Re-Edit
15. Bicep - Sundial
16. Erin McCarley - Into the Fire
17. Hayley Williams - Just A Lover
18. Jonas Blue - Something Stupid (feat. AWA)
19. Taylor Swift - Lover
20. Bebe Rexha - I'm Gonna Show You Crazy
21. Bea Miller - S.L.U.T.
22. The Pussycat Dolls - I Don't Need A Man
23. Kelly Rowland - Work - Freemasons Radio Edit
24. Gwen Stefani - Slow Clap
25. London Grammar - How Does It Feel - Paul Woolford Remix

26. Hayley Williams - Colour Me In
27. Lindsey Stirling - Lose You Now - Acoustic
28. Aly & Fila - Somebody Loves You - Paul Thomas Remix
29. Shanti Dope - Amatz
30. Kat Meoz - Whatever I Want
31. Kat Meoz - Never Back Down
32. Billie Eilish - Your Power
33. Yung Bae - Woman On The Moon (feat. UPSAHL)
34. WILLOW - t r a n s p a r e n t s o u l feat. Travis Barker
35. Angels & Airwaves - Rebel Girl
36. Lilith Czar - Anarchy
37. The Offspring - Let The Bad Times Roll
38. The Band CAMINO - 1 Last Cigarette
39. Wolf Alice - Smile
40. YONAKA - Call Me a Saint
41. You Me At Six - WYDRN
42. First to Eleven - Bye Bye Bye
43. VÉRITÉ - by now (stripped)
44. UPSAHL - Douchebag
45. SOAK - Blud
46. P!nk - Cover Me In Sunshine
47. You Me At Six - Voicenotes - Alternative Version
48. JOSEPH - Fighter
49. Pep Squad - Live For This - Remix
50. Christian Reindl - Home
51. Judith Hill - The Other Side
52. H.E.R. - Fate
53. Claire Guerreso - We Were Born for This
54. Neoni - Bloodstream
55. Klergy - As We Fall
56. DREAMERS - Palm Reader - All Time Low Remix
57. Billie Eilish - Lost Cause
58. SVRCINA - Effortless

59. Klergy - And so It Begins
60. ADONA - Dark Things
61. Alice Boman - Wish We Had More Time
62. The Pussycat Dolls - Buttons - Final Edit Version
63. Nothing But Thieves - Futureproof
64. Olivia O'Brien - No More Friends (with Oli Sykes of Bring Me The Horizon)
65. Garbage - Wolves
66. YONAKA - Raise Your Glass
67. YONAKA - Ordinary
68. YONAKA - Seize the Power
69. The Kills - Cosmic Dancer
70. Bexley - If We Have to Die
71. D'Arcy Spiller - Wolf Blood
72. Saint Agnes – Vampire
73. Lilith Czar - King
74. Eve - Tambourine - Edited Version
75. Dixie - FUCKBOY

Roman

1. Story Untold - i luv that u hate me
2. Joyeur - Dig
3. The Black Keys - Howlin' For You
4. Mumford & Sons - The Wolf
5. Kat Cunning - Supernova (tigers blud) (with PVRIS) - PVRIS Remix
6. Holy Wars - Welcome to My Hell
7. The Black Keys - Keep My Name Outta Your Mouth
8. Dead Poet Society - .burymewhole. - Single Version
9. 8 Graves - Teeth
10. Cemetery Sun - Fake Love
11. Dead Poet Society - CoDA
12. Demob Happy - Autoportrait
13. Fight The Fade - Devil
14. Big Spring - Shovel It In
15. Call Me Karizma - Rockstar
16. Tate McRae - Heather - Spotify Singles
17. Ingrid Andress - Don't Start Now
18. Pale Waves - You Don't Own Me
19. N.E.R.D - Rock Star
20. M.I.A. - Paper Planes
21. Florence + The Machine - Howl
22. Evanescence - Better Without You
23. The Pale White - That Dress
24. Everything Everything - SUPERNORMAL
25. Foxes - Amazing
26. Royal Blood - Limbo
27. Little Simz - Introvert
28. CHVRCHES - He Said She Said
29. The Hunna - Bad Place
30. The Pale White - Sonder
31. Fink - Warm Shadow - IIUII Edit

32. LŪN - demolition (Ruined by Glass Petals)
33. Monster Magnet - Learning to Die
34. Bicep - Hawk
35. Joan Smith & the Jane Does - Pull
36. Secrecies - So Quickly
37. Bjéar - Hymn
38. Frank Carter & The Rattlesnakes - My Town (feat. Joe Talbot)
39. Stand Atlantic - deathwish (feat. nothing,nowhere.)
40. Dropkick Murphys - Turn Up That Dial
41. Royal Blood - Oblivion
42. Angels & Airwaves - The Adventure
43. The Cure - Just like Heaven - 2006 Remaster
44. While She Sleeps - NERVOUS
45. Chris Daughtry - Bring Me To Life
46. Zero 9:36 - Adrenaline
47. Escape the Fate - Invincible (feat. Lindsey Stirling)
48. All Time Low - Once In A Lifetime
49. Inhaler - Cheer Up Baby
50. Beartooth - The Past Is Dead
51. Sullivan King - Venomous (feat. Spencer Charnas of Ice Nine Kills)
52. Badflower - F*ck The World
53. Twenty One Pilots - Saturday
54. Sum 41 - Catching Fire (feat. nothing,nowhere.)
55. Tom Odell - lose you again
56. U2 - Song For Someone
57. Rich Aucoin - Reset
58. The Amazons - In My Mind
59. Jung Youth - What The Game's Been Missing
60. NOISY - Days Go By
61. Fozzy - Sane - Radio Edit
62. Tommee Profitt - Sinner & Saint
63. Calvin Harris - By Your Side (feat. Tom Grennan)
64. Zayde Wølf - New Blood (Reimagined)

65. Norman - Here We Go
66. UNSECRET - No Good
67. UPSAHL - Melatonin
68. Inhaler - It Won't Always Be Like This
69. Bring Me The Horizon - Steal Something.
70. Garbage - Godhead
71. Anavae - Trippin'
72. Hooligan Hefs - SEND IT! (feat. Tinie Tempah) - Remix
73. SVRCINA - Closer to You
74. John Legend - Conversations in the Dark
75. Jill Andrews - Get up, Get On

ABOUT THE AUTHOR

Susan Harris is a writer from Cork, Ireland and when she's not torturing her readers with heart-wrenching plot twists or killer cliffhangers, she's probably getting some new book related ink, binging her latest TV or music obsession, or with her nose in a book.

Susan LOVES connecting with her fans!
www.susanharrisauthor.com

www.ingramcontent.com/pod-product-compliance
Lightning Source LLC
Chambersburg PA
CBHW020408210626
46816CB00006BB/2170